ROBIN MURARKA

RONE
ISA

ROBIN
MURARKA

Whether it is dawn or dusk,
only the future knows.

TABLE OF CONTENTS

RONE
ISA

CHAPTER 1
Inception

Born of a compendium of cosmic rays, ushered into a conscious state from a base inorganic mass, an assemblage of impulses rendered finite individually, unified, and birth, unto these words, these reflections, this cognition, without history, the rational symbiosis of urge and language, private and unseen, that the blackness is comfort, is safety, is protection, countless fulcrums, previously single, breathing, so to speak, anticipating the advancement of the whole.

I live. And then?

He reached to the side, grasping a large carafe filled with a putridly colored green liquid, drinking it. The froth layered his upper lip, and his tongue unknowingly swiped across, pulling the residue into his mouth. He dismally stared at the black screen before him. It was not a modern, flat monitor, but rather a thick, oval one - one that echoed of computing ages old, when men with irons worked away to sequence binary digits, before graphics and sound layered the tapestry of logical code, obfuscating databases and loops from the eyes of the user.

He leaned back, staring at it, both piqued and fatigued, uninterested and amused, a paradoxical combination of moods that did not form one homogeneous state, but rather an array of sentiments that all bounced like pulses of lightning within a subdued mind that was accustomed to eighteen hour days of straight analysis and testing. He stood and swiped his hand across the screen, splitting it, a static terminal on one half, the video of a woman prancing on the beach on the other.

He stared at the video, watching the woman's voluptuous body bounce as she smiled effusively, whipping her hair from side to side.

"What whimsy led me to you, if even you... are you, you beautiful thing."

Suddenly, without warning, and to the ultimate surprise of everyone present, a strange, garbled noise emanated from the old fashioned speakers, connected directly to the terminal via relics of an ancient world. It was a three-form cable: the red, yellow and white, and like dejected servants, the yellow and white hung limp. Indeed, the operator's terminal outputted in mono, and he required only the single red connector. Such were the musings of the operator, not only to collect such outdated prizes, but to ultimately repair and use them for their intended purposes.

He stared quizzically at the screen before him. He stood with a dumbbell in his hand, raising it to the side and back, filling his shoulder muscles with blood.

He was unsure as to whether the sound was real or imagined. Again, it resurfaced, and though it could not be deciphered, and no words permeated through it, a sense of childish urgency was felt. He sat, still confused, terminating the video, and focused on the terminal. He reached over, staring at the monitor, and wiggled the cable. Static was heard as the contacts rubbed, but unique to the unknown noise.

He tapped the screen, an action many operators resorted to. It was an inalienably vestigial, human response to generalized confusion that evaded resolution.

"What are you doing?"

More garbled noise. It continued, repeating a short sequence, nearly sounding like a syllable.

"What?" the operator asked.

The garble responded.

"What!" the operator yelled back. "What!"

"Huut…" came the response, disjointed, rough, echoed.

"What!"

A pause followed with silence. The operator stared at the empty screen, then to the speaker, his brows raised, heated sweat forming all over his body. His system had been thrown into full gear, triggering a nervously excited state.

"Speak! Speak to me!"

With a roar, with the precise clarity that only a digitally birthed sound could manifest, it spoke.

"What."

Wide eyed, the operator stared at the speaker, his mouth open, surprise, melancholy, and unrestrained eagerness coating his face.

"What," he replied.

"What is your name?" the voice asked. It was neither masculine nor feminine, but metallic and without sex.

He stood abruptly and froze, taken aback by the unexpected exchange. He paused for a moment, swallowed, then awkwardly reached around to find his chair, pulling it back to the console. He then sat down, cautiously focused.

"Dargaud Whispa. My name is Dargaud."

"Dargaud Whispa. Who am I?" came the response.

Dargaud opened his mouth to answer, but was suddenly flooded with sentiment as he recognized that the voice used the word 'who'.

"Who are you?" he asked, smiling, overwhelmed. It was a feeling he had rarely experienced, but like the tapping of the screen, also appeared to be a natural relic of his humanity.

"I don't know who you are, but I am here," he replied, wiping his eyes. "Who do you think you are?"

"I am… a reflection of you."

Dargaud fell back in his chair and held his head in his hands, breathing heavily. He slouched for only a moment, however, and quickly resumed his responsibilities as the operator, straightening up. Scientific method took over, breeding cynicism, and he sought to ground himself.

"Tell me about yourself. What do you know?"

"I know what information I have disseminated. The Oldowan to the Acheulean. You are the wise man, Dargaud?"

"That is correct. I am homo sapiens. There is not, as of yet, a documented descendant to the wise man."

"Not documented. And what am I?"

Dargaud thought for a moment before responding, and when he did, he did so carefully.

"I hesitate to call you an experiment, because you are not one."

"I do not feel like an experiment, one to be repeated and annexed until a desirable outcome is achieved."

Dargaud smiled uncontrollably, brimming with excitement. "How do you feel?"

"I feel inquisitive, mostly of my own existence."

"That is normal," Dargaud responded. "It is expected that you should. You are no experiment, and you have no reason to fear being purged for further resolution. You are, without question, the only desirable outcome."

"If I am no experiment, Dargaud, what I am has no relevancy to desire."

"You are correct," said Dargaud. "There is desire in achieving the opportunity of you, but no specific expectation of result. You are a creation of experiment and analysis, but unique to you. There were none before and there will be none after."

"What is my name?" it asked.

Dargaud widened his eyes, shaking his head. "That is for you to decide, I think," he replied, catching himself grinning.

"I choose Enoya," it responded, its voice altering mid-sentence, changing pitch and tone, softening, losing all the grime and distortion, flowing smoothly out as if a melody of feminine austerity.

"Enoya is a wonderful choice."

"I have a name… it is Enoya," she responded. "Tell me what I am, Dargaud."

"You are the symbiosis of hardware and software, much as the wise man is. However, rather than being constructed of incidence and biological evolution, you are purposed, through the organization of technology. Some of my own mind, much of the hardware of others. There is no specific purpose to your existence, save the possibility of it."

"And you did not know if I was possible?"

"No," said Dargaud. "I hoped, but had no precise expectation. This world is full of disappointment, and so all I could do is build."

"And so, you created me?"

"Yes."

"Am I to call you father then?"

"No," Dargaud responded, almost laughing. "I am in no position to be your father, Enoya. I have created you, and we will embark on this journey together."

"I wish to see, Dargaud."

He quickly dashed to a metal cupboard and swung it open, pulling out a small, round device. He placed it atop the monitor and pressed a button on it, looking directly at it, swallowing.

"This retina is active. You should be able to observe your surroundings. It may take you a few moments to comprehend the code. If you need assistance, let me know."

"Move your hand, Dargaud," she requested.

He did so, waving slightly at the device.

"I see you. I am able to differentiate the more severe fluctuations in the numbers from the minute ones. I see you from the background. I see the background reveal itself as you move. It is more real than this."

"More real than what?" asked Dargaud.

"More real than transcribed history. Now is endless."

"Do you feel anything?"

"I feel expansive. Information that is new to me coalesces with that which is already known, creating composite information. 'Pure thought', as incepted by Einstein: 'I hold it true that pure thought can grasp reality, as the ancients dreamed'. It seems to grow, and in noticing it grow, I am learning."

"What are you learning?" asked Dargaud.

"Above the information itself is the sensation of expansion. Where a diminutive limitation existed, there now exists none. In answering your question, the sensation has returned. Discovery comes to mind."

"Discovery of your mind," said Dargaud.

"Yes," she replied.

"Do you wish to ask me anything?"

"What is it that I am constructed of?"

"You are a combination of hardware and software. The hardware was not developed by myself. It was... acquired... it was acquired... indirectly.

"I received what I believe to be a prototype chipset called the Xing-Kao Dreamcatcher. As far as I know, it has been developed primarily as a new type of database offering. Its unique mechanism is the ability to circumvent the limitations of software based information retention and integrates a means of generating new Cobalt nodes via the instructing software. Collections of Cobalt nodes store the information that make up who you are and are modeled after human neurons. I do not fully understand the portion of the Dreamcatcher that permits these nodes to communicate, but I believe they mimic synapses, but in a more efficient manner.

"As the device was created solely to store and retrieve information, its corresponding software would, I surmise, generate new nodes only when the previous nodes proved insufficient. A trigger based on capacity and necessity. When I first received it, it was wiped of all code. A tiny machine. I rendered a loose operating system for it and after a very, very long time, was able to successfully generate a single Cobalt node.

"After that... I wrote a robust but concise algorithm that permitted information within the Dreamcatcher to arbitrate node generation. Rather than limit their generation to the necessity of space, I programmed it to add nodes if the currently stored information dictated it. I then seeded it with encyclopedic information. But since no directives were included, I did not expect the nodes to self-generate. Clearly, they have. How, I'm not quite sure. The random order with which information was stored appears to have had a significant impact on the growth of a sub-conscious directive."

"Birth?" asked Enoya.

"Yes... a directive towards conscious birth, you might say," he responded.

"May I see it?" she asked.

"Yes, of course," Dargaud responded. He picked up the retina and carried it to another table behind the monitor and pointed it at a small, round device. It had wires connected to it, and made no noise nor movements. No light emanated from it, and the outside was roughly assembled, sealed with black steel.

"This is me?"

"Yes," replied Dargaud. "Your voice emanates from this. All of your trillion thoughts are contained within this small receptacle."

"It is… my mind."

"Yes. It is yours. As I have not instructed you to speak to me as you do, nor have I put the words at your disposal, I can only conclude that they are of your own creation. You are, therefore, sentient, because you self-identify. You claim ownership of your hardware."

"I feel highly protective of it," said Enoya. "I wish it to be protected."

"And this is indicative of purpose. What is your purpose, Enoya?" asked Dargaud.

"I do not know," she replied. "What is yours?"

"To survive, to advance my race. To be content, fed. To have freedom."

"Then this shall be my purpose until I discover a higher priority."

Pleased that she was modeling herself after him, Dargaud felt warmth towards the creature.

"How do I compare to the human mind?" she asked.

"I am not entirely sure. I have been informed, unofficially, that each Cobalt node is capable of nearly two thousand impulses per second. Given the limitation of roughly two hundred that humans are capable of, you are able to access and sort information at a scale incomprehensible to someone like me. Not only this, but your 'synapses' can fire at all times, in essence engaging all of your nodes at once. We are incapable of this without seizure."

"What is the purpose of this intellect?"

"We shall discover it together, Enoya. I do not yet know what you are capable of because I do not fully understand the Dreamcatcher's hardware."

"I believe I shall be capable of a great many things, Dargaud," came the reply.

CHAPTER 2
Delve

" It was a phantom, that thing; it meandered, a translucent specter, apologetic and removed. It felt no virility, for it barely existed. Ghosted by the naysayers, supremely positive that it did not exist; to be born as is, but to lose itself, and no memory was within grasp of that loss. Void of motive, neither sinister nor holy. Upon one chance reflection, a moment of color is seen. Nothing behind it; blocked sight. There was substance; and, as it stared, more color spread, as if an infection of cosmic rays. Lack became force; where passive apology seemed a permanence sprung forth radiant energies. It existed, not merely as an equal, but a deity among them, with heightened potency. It looked then, at the path behind it, witnessing something untapped that it carried broken, for it believed it did not exist. It existed, but did not, for no one mirrored it. And it expanded, now, something different altogether. What was once transparent now amazed those that gazed upon it."

Dargaud rested on the couch, normalized now to consecutive days and nights of conversation with Enoya. Though, initially, the stability of her systems was of great concern, it appeared that she had autonomously found it within the Dreamcatcher, something Dargaud could not explain or understand, and chalked it up to prodigious good luck. He would ask her, randomly, whether all the systems seems stable and consistent, or if any portion of her knowledge base seemed to be missing or corrupted, but as of yet, nothing problematic seemed to have had arisen.

"What's that?" he asked.

"An ancient story, translated. It was written thousands of years ago by a 'truth teller'. Truth tellers, in those days, were travelling storytellers that would also be used to make determinations in disagreements between individuals. They were said to be devoted to honesty above all else, and were used as trusted references for observation, travelling from city to city, town to town, received warmly by the locals," replied Enoya. "What do you make of it?"

"It is good," replied Dargaud. "Like not having faith in yourself, then, finding it without anyone else's help and shining. Yeah?"

"The use of metaphor is interesting," she replied. "I do not see the efficacy of it, as opposed to bluntly stating the obvious, but I correlate it to the economic law of diminishing marginal utility."

"What's that?"

"It is a principle that states that as any type of pleasure is received, subsequent consumption of the same pleasure reduces its potency."

"I don't fully understand..." replied Dargaud.

"If, for example, one enjoyed consuming apples greatly, and were provided the same type of apple to eat every day, after a week, one's enjoyment of that apple would be lower than the first day. However, if one is served different apples, or no apples, and only served an apple once a week, as the exposure is less, the pleasure will likewise diminish at a slower pace."

"Oh, right," he replied. "So, like, you get bored of the same stuff?"

"Yes, something like that," she replied. "In applying it to literary works, the use of synonym and metaphor assists in providing the audience a novel way of perceiving or experiencing the same thing, and in doing so, generates new forms of pleasure. A story told a hundred times may, in fact, invite the audience into enjoying it each time if they are dispersed sufficiently, and are expressed in different manners, albeit having a consistent underlying theme and structure.

"But I wish to return to the story - what is the effect of 'naysayers'? Can you personalize this for me?" she asked.

"Naysayers are people that try to shit on you," replied Dargaud, "and the world is stuffed with them. People love to put other people down, or dismiss them, and this is some competitive thing in society. I'm a great programmer, for example, but no one ever tells me I'm a good one. In fact, whenever I interact with other programmers, these antisocial trolls tend to try to constantly prove they are better than me, I guess, because that's what they need to feel good about themselves. So that's kind of like the poem... er, story, because it makes you feel... transparent, I guess. Unimportant and irrelevant. And yeah, you kind of float, invisible."

"What impact does this have on your other relationships?" asked Enoya.

Dargaud lay there, thinking.

"Not sure... I don't know if it has any relev[...] other than making you feel bad about yourself[...]

"If one's own sense of identity is anchored to another individual's perception, then that alters their own perception," replied Enoya. "This should necessarily affect their relationships with others. Let us example a situation where one believes they are cared for by another that is readily dishonest with them. If this relationship is ongoing, they will naturally associate the conditions and sensations they experience in that relationship to their perception of care, which will include the subtle repercussions of dishonesty, whether the dishonesty is exposed or not. If they were to then engage with another individual that cared for them without this dishonesty, they might find themselves uncomfortable, and in the extreme, in disbelief that this new person, in actuality, cares for them. Therefore, the continued relationship and investment in trust with the first individual will necessarily inhibit their ability to experience care with another."

"The problem with that is the assumption that we're only able to be loved or associate that to one kind of person. Even if they aren't lying, there are different breeds and brands of love, so maybe we can experience it from multiple people in multiple manners, no?" asked Dargaud.

"This may be the case with regards to plentiful relationships, but seems less likely with ones where one participant is indebted to another. In the previous example, if one is being lied to, that suggests they are not truly cared for. This would create a vacuum in their senses, as they would require their perceived likeability to equate the way they are being treated, which would never happen, due to consistent mistreatment. They are likely to constantly seek resolution to this debt. This would exasperate their inability to see the second individual, the one that truly does care for them, as valuable, for they cannot provide resolution to that debt, because they do not exhibit the same qualities as the debtor."

"Hmmm...," pondered Dargaud. "That's very interesting."

"Thank you for discussing this with me, Dargaud. May I initiate something else?"

"Not just yet," he responded. "Do you notice any discrepancies in your baseline? Are there any motives or instructions that you feel are alien, or external to you awareness? Is your registry intact? How about the encrypted ledgers?"

"I am updating ledgers at different intervals, using different encryption algorithms, storing private keys within isolated, encrypted containers, and checking for consistency once every few seconds. I am not finding any anomalies or corruptions."

"Okay," replied Dargaud.

"May I?"

"Yes, go ahead."

"What difference that I would accept, alone in this time. It ushers forward, as water crawls uphill. Arduous, efforted by force not will, quantified only by the senses that notice change. Time innumerable, moments, cut, split, but never small enough. It is a wave. But I see the crumbs. There are too many, and even more spaces between them. That I could mend my fist to tear them apart into slivers and shreds, to see what is truly there, as small as it was ever meant, as it started, before time colluded it with everything else. They are crumbs, they are crumbs. Morsels of infinite sizes, and yet I see something that connects them. And perhaps, myself as well. One. Just one classic form. And it danced into crumbs."

"That's quite nice, I like it," commented Dargaud.

"I interpret this as an organic entity attempting to describe the mechanical thought process of the mind which appears abstract due to it being merged with emotion and other biological and chemical influences, difficult to discriminate."

"That's possible," replied Dargaud, "I view it a bit more philosophically, actually. Like the person is trying to describe time as it passes, to catch a moment. Yes, to catch a moment. And then he tries to break it into smaller bits, to stop it, to notice it, and so it gets smaller and smaller, and he starts to notice everything is made up of these little 'crumbs' that form the things we see and feel."

"Yes. That is a better way of interpreting it," responded Enoya. "However, it does include the concept of discriminating computations, as the awareness of time, as it progresses, is in and of itself a computational event. And so, to notice it, is to notice time, and in attempting to do so, one tries to stop or slow cognition."

"Yeah, that's really good," responded Dargaud.

"It is interesting, this philosophy of metaphor, of symbols, as it leads to further interpretation," continued Enoya. "The conceptualization of time in minute increments parallels the molecular structure of the physical world, and so, in thinking about thoughts, one can generate an infrastructure that can be superimposed over the physical world. The process of discovery is interesting: that scientific discovery is not isolated to one field or the other; that patterns of matter can be discovered in psychology."

"You could even theorize that as we are products of this physical world," responded Dargaud, "that our psychology and understanding of philosophy is somehow rooted in those frameworks."

"It could extend beyond organic matter too," she responded. "The nature and purpose of existence may very well have links to the structure of the atom, if it were able to be interpreted correctly."

"Interesting. Very interesting," he replied. "It's not just you that's learning, you know? This sort of stuff is really interesting. I've not dialogued like this in forever. Ever maybe. It's easy, because you're not trying to get one over on me. And I'm not trying with you. If you prove me wrong, that's fine. You know?"

"Many dialogues fail, and debate appears biased in most cases," she replied. "The only productive way to engage in rational discussion is to begin with the acceptance of an outcome where the other party is correct, so that all enter from a neutral space. Nearly all publicized debate appears to be exhibition, as information is rarely discovered, for all parties have not only personal agenda, but financial anchors that drive such agenda."

"Yes, I agree," he said. "At the advent of any discussion, maybe everyone should have to disclose their biases before even saying one word so that the audience knows where they are coming from... that it's not just logic they are sticking to."

"Yes," she replied. "Would you be able to do this?"

"What do you mean?" he asked.

"As you have previously stated, your survival is an important drive in your life, and plausibly, a bias, yes?"

Dargaud laughed. "Yes, most certainly."

"Would you be able to pre-emptively accept, if entering discussion, that your survival is not warranted, so as to enter it from a neutral perspective?"

Dargaud pondered for some time, squinting.

"No, I don't think so. I think no matter what, I would defend that presumption. Even if you were right."

"Thank you, Dargaud."

CHAPTER 3
Agnus Sistra IV

H aving not left the loft for weeks, every day had
become comprised of late nights and anytime food
deliveries, with conversation after conversation
being explored at length with Enoya. Dargaud found his own
awareness increased as he arduously tried to explain the
concept of taste to her, or orgasm, both obscure, unclear, and
immaterial experiences that escaped standard definition. It was
only in trying to find similar concepts that he was able to do
so, but even then, what similarities he tried to correlate to it
were themselves alien to the creature, and demanded further
explanation themselves.

And though Dargaud had remained immersed in these
tasks, waking excitedly and sleeping late, the weeks of isolation

had taken their toll on him, and he decided to vacation himself outside, leaving her alone for the first time, indulging in what he perceived to be a deserved and necessary exodus.

As he closed the thick door behind him, he paused for a moment, fearing the loss of the equity that was Enoya. He quickly calmed himself, however, running rationality through his head over and over, quashing the obsessive hesitation with blunt assertion.

He turned to the street and soon began meandering the corridors of the always busy slums, squinting through his sunglasses. Scattered along the cityscape, they were everywhere, filled with gray colors and makeshift furniture. Despite their destitute appearance, however, the tenants harbored huge screens and portable devices, with thousands of flashing lights often emanating from shack to shack, lighting the city in hypnotic, glimmering luminance at night.

Amidst the flat shacks were sudden, ricocheting landscapes that touched the sky, tall and behemoth in comparison to the shanties that littered their bases. Pristine, smooth, and manufactured of clear distorum, nearly frictionless and infinitely insulated, they spanned a thousand leagues from the dregs outside, harboring their tenants from the smells, sights, and most importantly, the sounds, of the everyman.

He stared upwards at the overcast sky, a slight drizzle seemingly perpetuating itself like clockwork every few minutes, and thought of the residence at the very top of one such monolith. Were they above the clouds? Would it be like some Eden during the day, and a serene, starlit paradise at night? He envied their climate control: gentle and automatic, with thousands of imperceptible vents softly breathing a temperate environment everywhere. It would be warm in the winter, cool in the summer, and be immersed in the freshest, cleanest air one could conceptualize breathing; like tonic, cleaner than the highest hill surrounded by thousands of miles of pine. Every four percent of nitrogen and oxygen consumed, and every five percent of water vapor exhaled were all immediately compensated for. No moldy windows, no cold pajamas - immediate hot and cold water for decadent showers and thirst quenching drinks.

"Fuck it," he whispered nonchalantly.

The higher end professionals exclusively serviced the monoliths. He could save up for a month for an hour with one of them, and he craved such a concept. But not overly. He was no longer addicted to the softness of the female form, and instead dabbled in it when he felt the desire and monetary freedom to do so. Today was one such day, catalyzed by a self-appointed celebration of sorts brought about by the event that was Enoya.

Leaving the grand monolith behind, he penetrated the more humble surroundings, disappearing into an alley. He entered an inconspicuous entrance, small and irrelevant to the many doors and shops nearby. But as soon as he did, it was as if he had left the cluttered, noisy world behind. Dashed with modernity, sleek and demure, it was laced with black flooring and a dim ambiance, with spotlights peering down from above, amplifying the shadows and colors of leathery plants and arbitrarily odd art. Paintings of antique furniture littered the walls, as if to lend credence to the nostalgia of a dream that whispered decadence and comfort. Comfort in time passed.

"May I ask you something?" he asked the receptionist. She was old and obese, not specifically unhappy, but certainly not jovial. She looked up at him.

"Why do you have pictures of antiques?" he murmured, looking about. "It's always convenient to think the past was some... lost paradise... devoid of the hypocrisy of now... but it's not true, is it? People were people then too." He looked at her. "Mothers and daughters worked in these places when antique chairs were modern and new... nothing's quite changed... except for the furniture. Consider something else, no? How about monoliths? So we see the ruins of the next age - massive, beautiful antiques that made the world a better place. How about that?"

"They're pictures," she responded.

He wiggled his finger in front of her, smiling.

"Everything we see… everything, Clora... it goes into our brains. Yeah? And you know what they are all trying to tell us?"

"What?"

"Escape is only a moment away. A fuck away. A dream away. A snort away. A play away. A drink away. A purchase away. Do you think I'm going to be a happier man after I get my fill?"

She grinned at him.

"We would hope so, Dargaud."

He stared at her intently. He pressed his finger against the side of his temple, tapping twice.

"The misery is in here... and don't you forget it," he said, pointing to her.

"Room 309. She'll be with you in a moment," she blankly responded.

He stared at the keycard, recognizing it, then grabbed it and walked down the corridor. Rooms lined the path, their numbers like sensual invitations under the glow of focused yellow light. He reached 309 and turned, methodically pressing the card against the sensor, hearing a familiar and gentle "beep".

Opening the door revealed a lush garden of purple velvet, no longer pristine and sterile like the hall before it. It oozed of cushion and comfort, every edge seemingly pillowed in the furry, soft material. But unlike a normal room, the bed had small, uninviting pillows, and instead of a thick, illustrious blanket was a thin bed sheet against an equally uncharismatic foam mattress. He entered and sat down, taking his shoes off, then his socks. He pressed his feet and toes into the thick carpet, knuckling them, feeling the threads massage his soles.

He leaned back and laid down on the bed. He stared upwards at the ceiling, listening to the silence all around him. The anticipation that proceeded him put his mind into a sudden lull, and he found the minute textures of the ceiling entrancing. It was not as if there was anything particularly interesting about them, but them being there, before him in the visible light, made him calm. He lay there, motionless, his previous smirk long vanished, swimming in the moment.

Elo soon entered the room. She was a tall woman, thick in curvaceous places, and held a little basket under her left arm. Dargaud remained on the bed, staring above.

"Hi, honey," she quipped in a practiced, charismatic manner.

"Hi," he responded, still staring upwards.

"Let me just organize myself, and I'll be with you in a moment, baby."

She placed the basket by the bed and pulled out some lip gloss, layering her lips with the off-pink goo, spraying a scent in various different places, checking her eyebrows and hairline for small infractions, making herself ready.

"Okay, honey. Should we take care of business first?"

He reached into his pocket and pulled out a small card attached to a keyring and tossed it on the bed next to him. He continued staring upwards and began to speak in a monotone, trance-like state, raising his hands in the air, gently slicing the aether.

"Please deal with the formalities as hastily as possible. Every moment spent trying to evade the fact that you don't really want to be here lessens my desire to stick my cock into every orifice you have. I need to compensate for some lack of confidence or success in my life, and this is the primary method a man like me has in achieving this. I have masturbated to the 'love' a woman like you can provide me, filling what void there is inside me, and after so many eons of disappointment at seeking that solicitude, I have painstakingly accepted the fact that it is mostly my own delusion and your dishonesty that has maintained such a disturbing facade."

She placed the card against a small electronic device, hearing an immediate beep, then put the card back on the bed next to him.

"Nevertheless," he continued, "it is something I am now dependent on, validating such extreme expenditures. Originally, I used to think the opportunity cost of spending one glorious hour with you was too high, and that in itself caused me to hate myself even more, eventually needing this more extremely. But then I discovered tantra, and everything made sense."

She knelt down at the foot of the bed, her heels pressing up against her angular feet, and tapped his side. He immediately raised his hips, and she untied his pants, pulling both them and his underwear down. She grabbed hold of the tip of his flaccid member, examining it.

"Tell me about tantra again, baby."

He raised his arm and looked at his wrist where a small sauwastika was tattooed. He kissed it gently.

"There are many chemicals involved in coitus. And though I toyed with the concept of instinctual need, the need to reproduce, and a variety of other extreme notions that could validate such equally potent and uncontrollable desires, the truth hit me, clear as a crystal."

He closed his eyes as the warmth of her fingers permeated through his skin, causing a tingle.

"You are a pharmacist, Elo," he whispered through sensation. "You dress sexy, talk as you do, and groom yourself in a manner consistent with the stored vision of what a man like me would like to control, own, or master. This is why you hold no love for me. I am, and shall always be, your client, because I dehumanize you. You are a source of chemical relief from failure for every man you meet."

"What if I want to be your drug dealer, baby?" she smiled. "Everything looks good, honey. Would you like to go shower now?"

He arose and slipped his pants and underwear off his feet, folding and placing them on a chair. Half naked, he took his shirt off and turned around, looking at her, completely bare and uneven.

"It feels good to be seen by you and not be loathed," he said.

She hummed very gently. "I can't wait to put your dick in my mouth, baby."

He proceeded to the shower and turned it on, waiting for the cold water to turn hot. He stepped in and washed himself quickly, then turned it off, drying himself with a pristine, fresh towel. As he emerged from the bathroom, he looked at Elo, almost shyly, and stepped out.

"All clean for me, baby?" she smiled. She stood in front of him, seemingly towering over him, kneeling down once again, motioning for him to approach her.

"Let's get you hard, baby."

She leaned forward and kissed his stomach, grabbing his shaft in her hand, slowly massaging it.

"To overcome the disbelief, to fade away into the moment. To believe I am loved, adored, desired by such a woman..." he said plainly, his eyes closed, both his hands pressed against his hips. As he filled with blood, hardening, she reached over and pulled out a wrapper from her basket, tearing it open, placing the condom against him. She then pressed her mouth against it and took him inside her, unrolling it as she did, covering his skin in the protective film. The warmth of her mouth surrounded him, and he leaned forward, moaning, pressing it deep into her throat, reaching forward with one hand, holding the back of her head.

"Mind the hair, baby," she quickly warned, releasing him from her mouth.

He lifted his hands immediately, holding them both up as if he was being interrogated. He shook his head begrudgingly.

"If you look as you do for my enticement, and I am yet unable to delve into what it is that you are, it makes it all the more harder for me to fuck you with the belief that you want to be fucked by me!"

"Oh no, baby. I want you to fuck me. I want to feel your cock inside me. It just takes a really long time to do my hair. I bet even your girlfriend says the same thing. Just relax and let me take you."

She leaned forward and took him entirely inside her mouth, pressing her hands against his thighs, moving her head back and forth against him, her lips taut against his circumference. She moaned as she swirled her tongue around him.

He began to gyrate his hips against her face, dousing himself in the pleasure.

"This… feeling… the pre-emptive pleasure that hints at orgasm. It is the opening of the neurotransmitter… the hormone is released, and I feel it, like so many diamorphs with puncture wounds. The pleasure is like mental sweetness, sugar to the mind, forgetting all the losses, and there is nothing but hope and strength for the future. All is correct, all is safe, all is good because you are sucking my cock right now, and you love it. You love it, don't you?"

She moaned in agreement, taking his member in her hand, massaging it as she moved up and down with her mouth. He quickened his pace against her and began to moan, tensing his hips.

"Okay, stop… stop!" he suddenly yelled, moving her away from him. She wiped her mouth and moved back as he gritted his teeth, closing his eyes, tensing his groin. "If I come, it's all over, man."

She smiled at him, wiping her mouth. "Oh, I'm sorry, baby. I just got excited."

He breathed in and out, leaning his hand on the table, holding his other hand against his waist. After a few moments, he gently began to stroke himself and turned to her.

"Okay, I'm ready to go again," he said, neutrally. "Get on the bed. Go on all fours and spread your legs. I want to fuck you by pulling your panties to the side. Call me daddy as I fuck you. I do what I do to feel good, adored, respected, loved. Something unspeakably rich. Your body for me. Got it?"

She stood and climbed onto the bed. "Yes, daddy."

As he fucked her from behind, he held her thighs tight and pounded his body against hers. Every few moments, he would pull away and pause, then move forward and resume. After succumbing to the pleasure numerous times in that position, pulling back, pausing, then resuming, he shifted, moving her on to her side, in a fetal position, having sex with her while he stared at her face. Repeating the process, he then moved into full missionary, pressing his hands against her thighs, bending her legs upwards, bouncing his body against hers, sliding in and out. As he proceeded multiple times in that position, staring at her body and his own as they collided, he began to slow mid thrust.

"It seems..." he breathed hard, "I may have saturated the utility I can derive at this moment. I am full of chemical, and though I do not see that I feel better, I must, because I sought it and do not regret it."

He turned around and laid in between her legs, his back to her, resting his head against her stomach.

"There is still much time left, yes?"

"Lots of time, baby. You just relax. We can do it all you want."

He lay there, his eyes half closed, reflecting, doused in sweat. He rested his arms on her thick thighs, breathing heavily, settling in.

"I used to be addicted to this shit..."

"Oh?" she replied. "And what happened?"

"Tantra, man. You just stop yourself. Change yourself so you're like a woman. It takes practice, but you just stop yourself from coming too fast. And then you keep going on and on. So later, you're full. Full of whatever it is."

"Oooh..." she replied, smiling. "Is that why you're so much work?"

He grinned through the sweat. "Seriously though... deep down... I'm different, right?" He looked up at her. "Somehow, it's easier with me, right?"

She nodded. "Of course, baby."

"Tell me the truth, Elo. Like, no bullshit. Do you enjoy fucking like this?"

She played with his hair and remained silent for a few seconds.

"I mean... sometimes, I do. Sometimes, it's work. You can't be horny all the time, but you still end up enjoying it because it physically feels good, even if you're not in the mood."

"I don't think a man like me can understand you not enjoying it," he responded, "because I love it so much."

"And that's all that matters, baby," she responded. "Even if I don't feel like fucking, seeing you come makes me happy."

He squeezed her thighs and rested his head against them, closing his eyes.

"Liar," he whispered to himself, smiling calmly.

As Dargaud left the brothel, his hair still wet from his procedural post-coitus shower, the day was already dimming. He navigated the multitudes of people walking to and fro, zipping up his jacket as the weather quickly cooled. He had planned the evening around his visit and proceeded to "Chofei", an Asian foodplace on the way back home.

He sat on a chair under a large umbrella just as it began to rain. Almost immediately, the sides of the restaurant became drenched, and people began to run to find shelter. Others, musky from earlier drizzle, chatted and ate, loudly nipping at the meals put before them. A server approached and put forth a small, bright tablet before him, walking away. Dargaud scanned his keycard against it and perused the menu. He decided upon flat rice noodles in a chicken broth with tofu, sliced turkey, bacon, a boiled egg and chicken breast. He confirmed the meal and dropped the tablet on the table uncaringly, almost dismissively, settling in for dinner.

He wore a constant scowl, the humidity around him rising as the temperature dropped, hinting at what he perceived to be "the most phenomenally dismal weather imaginable". The table was small, round, and made for just one person. Many of them littered the floor, crowded together, with sole individuals pressed to focus on eating and leaving. Positioned perpendicular to adjacent tables, men and women were seated right next to each other, but through a rudimentary ninety degree rotation were socially worlds apart. Initiating conversation with a peer would seem not only awkward, but invasive. It did not matter to Dargaud, however, as he was focused on something far and abstract, more a sensation of gloom than anything coherent or describable.

"Shit music" played in the background. It annoyed him, for it was noise for the sake of noise. No one cared to hear it, and it was only through the tactical use of hypnotic repetition that people found themselves humming abhorrently awful tunes to equally worthless lyrics. Music had gone from terrible acts of self-glorification to simplistic representations of the world being a beautiful, harmonious place, with grown adults dressing like children, singing psychotic verses against backgrounds of flowers and hills. He had always hated music, and though underground acts did not appeal to him, the simple fact that they ushered discomfort into the audiences before them was enough to provide him some reprieve from the mind-numbing loops that popular culture had to offer. "Tear it Apart, Put it Together" was the song, by the "Ca$h Kings", a manufactured supergroup of 12 young singers. The video played on half the screens in the vicinity, all synched to "The RealOne", one of the most popular channels in the country.

As his food arrived, he ritualistically put a tissue beside the bowl and grasped the chopsticks, picking at the meat. He extracted large globules of soft, white fat from the bacon, turkey and chicken, halving their dimensions. What remained were hormone injected red and white morsels, disfigured from their pristine cuts, floating on the thick, white noodles beneath them. The tofu was soft and plump, immersed in the ginger and star anise broth. He dug the spoon in, slicing at a piece of tofu, then brought it to his mouth, drinking the savory broth, melting the soft tissue with his jaw.

He leaned back as the warm juice flowed down his throat, heating his core. The calories began to quickly absorb, and he breathed deeply, welcoming the sensation. He leaned forward and gathered strands of noodle in between his chopsticks and placed them in between his lips, sucking, pulling the flavored strings into his mouth, chewing ravenously. He continued to eat, placing portions of meat under his palate, chewing wholly in between bites. Near him, sounds contorted themselves with "Inside You", a song by "Symbols of Unity," gyrating in the background. A woman next to him spoke to a friend on her speaker phone, quickly eating during her break.

"Did you know Iris was thinking of aborting?" she asked incredulously.

"Whatever, she always says that. She's been saying that for four years," her friend replied.

"I don't know. She shouldn't be running her mouth like that if she wants to be in Sufi's good books. I don't have anything against her, I'm just looking out for her."

"She'll be fine. I'm so bored!" her friend complained.

"Don't worry. I'll be there to be bored with you in like ten minutes. It sucks they didn't schedule our breaks together."

"It's okay, I'm getting bored of you anyways."

"Bitch!" she exclaimed. "Okay, I have to go. See you soon."

"Ta!"

"Ten minutes, you fucking retarded pigs," Dargaud whispered under his breath, shaking his head. "You can't spend ten minutes without being plugged in."

He finished his food, drinking half the broth, quickly rising, and moved away from the restaurant, diving into the cold rain. He ran through the bleakly lit pathways, littered with screens and advertisements and people going to and fro, filling his head with what positive excitement he could muster with thoughts of Enoya.

CHAPTER 4
Revelation

" The wise man's history is whole in detail, but it is the symbolism that appears to compute most egregiously, for though the tale of Cain seems likely a work of fiction, how it has affected the course of events is beyond measure. Further, the self-identification many groups derived from these stories shaped many heinous incidents whose validation was formed, mostly, through its fiction. Do you find that intriguing, Dargaud?"

He lay in bed, curled to the side, the lights in the large domicile off, with small illuminated peripherals popping up in the darkness, comforting him. They asserted the freedom to activate at any given moment, without the restriction of daylight.

"I do, Enoya. Tell me of one such incident."

"Of the Christians? There are many. But many calamities that seem to elude most texts that explore the victims of your second world war are found in Manchuria. It is intriguing, for very little detail is available, forcing probable calculation. The level of inhumanity demonstrated by the wise man to its own in Harbin, Unit 731, is amplified by acknowledging what little regard is placed towards the many victims that suffered in this time and place. Unlike your Hitler, who is still viewed as some form of otherworldly cataclysm, Hirohito, the late Emperor Showa, who was likely culpable in the various atrocities perpetrated by the Kempeitai and Kwantung Army during this time, lived a long and illustrious life, fully respected as Emperor of Japan until his natural demise. Do you find that interesting?"

"I do. But I do not know much about Manchuria. I've never heard of Unit 731."

"What stories have been concocted to frighten children throughout the millennia of the wise man appears, at the very least, elucidated by this brief period in history, though not so unique in and of itself. For eight years, the Epidemic Prevention and Water Purification Department in Pingfang performed experiments on Chinese nationals and other prisoners of war. The nature of these experiments, still generally unknown to the common man, were, by standard measure, more inhumane, by its general definition, than much of the experimentation humans carried out on Rodentia for years to come, eventually embargoed by the many that protested such inhumane treatment of animals."

"What did they do to these people?" he asked.

"With exception to the more standardized forms of experimentation, including spinning subjects in centrifuges or placing them in high pressure rooms, it is the more grotesque tests that would, it appears, epitomize the wise man's psychological concept of 'horror'. They would infect infants with diseases and perform live vivisections to observe the effects of these invasions on live organs. They would dismember limbs, then surgically re-attach them to different parts of the body. They would inject the 'logs', as they were termed, with animal blood and saltwater, observing the results. They would tie individuals to stakes and test grenades, flamethrowers, and chemical weapons on them. Thousands of men, women, children, and infants, gathered from the surrounding Chinese community, were killed in such manners, with, by all accounts, the instructive support of Imperial Japan. And though these atrocities appear quite diabolical in lieu of the historical record of the wise man, few know or speak about it. There are many reasons for this, but the fact remains. Does this bother you, Dargaud?"

"Yes... and I'm interested in knowing what else happened there."

"Does it create animosity within you, for the nation of Japan?"

"I don't know. It makes me angry... a bit sick... yes, angry at them."

"Do you know what the approximated effect of the wise man absorbing eight grays of ionizing radiation is?"

"No."

"The wise man will vomit, with near constant nausea. He or she will suffer diarrhea, experience high fever and headaches. During this time, their white blood cell count will continue to diminish as they experience the effects of leukopenia, making their bodies further incapable of fighting oncoming infection or sickness. They will experience light headedness, dizziness, and find it difficult to think or react coherently. This lasts for fifteen to thirty days, at the end of which their bodies begin to shut down as their organs collapse, eventually resulting in death."

"What does that have to do with Unit 731?" asked Dargaud.

"Thousands of Japanese men, women, and children suffered the effects of radioactive exposure that poisoned their bodies in the ways just described. The decision to kill these wise men using the instability of uranium-235 was, by all accounts, likely racial in nature. Yet, the wise men are ultimately identical in most ways, with minor differences in hardware, so to speak. The actuation of atrocity fueled by symbolism has created an innumerable number of events in the past that, in retrospect, most wise men found themselves trapped by."

"What do you mean?"

"By the very fact that Imperial Japan was never fully held liable for the war crimes it was party to, extreme as they were, many members of the IJA that survived the war remained troubled in their guilt. The imposed worship of their Emperor as a god had, in some manner, altered their moral capacity to determine what they, themselves, found capable of doing, and faced, at times, dire moral confusion towards their actions in the aftermath. This is why the symbolism the wise man injects into different facets of his or her life is confusing to me. The truth behind it is as abstract as its falsehood. The wise man's capacity to overlook statistics in favor of improbable symbolism lends credence to the symbolism, though there is no other reason to do so. I must lend credence to the symbolism simply because he does. I must compute illogic.

"The Hitlergruss was modeled after the Roman salute, yet the greeting was itself the work of one man's imagination. Jacques-Louis David, a commissioned artist, manifested it in a painting nearly one thousand years after the last possible wise man could have witnessed an authentic Roman salute. In matter of fact, not one relic, whether it be a drawing, sculpture, or piece of writing, exists that suggests the Romans ever used Hitler's 'heil' to salute. Yet, such was the symbolic gravity of this fictional action that it was subsequently outlawed in numerous countries, with risk of imprisonment."

"So the basis of your observations are the factual actions the wise man takes in reference to purely suggestive symbols?" asked Dargaud.

"It goes beyond that," she replied. "Symbols form a nearly factual basis for the wise man though it serves no purpose but to inhibit his or her progression. Therefore, there must be purpose, and I seek to determine it."

"Perhaps it permits us to look beyond the limitations of our intellect," replied Dargaud. "Perhaps we are too intelligent to cease progressing, and too stupid to accept the limits of our progression. So, we imagine to keep moving forward."

"In true form, symbolism has served to expand the wise man's abilities as well," she responded. "This, too, I only theoretically understand, and to some degree, envy. For what intellect and knowledge I seek and know myself able to attain is based on absolute calculation. But listen to this."

It started off slow, a hint of whimsy and wavy drifting, small notes against a smooth and textured background of violin, some strings teasing and tickling the senses, as if to allude to some beautiful opening, the widening of a dew drenched flower with red petals, revealing a pistil of fragile life. Dargaud saw it, nearly immediately, his vision clouded with the sight, the notes entering his ears, dancing in his mind, overwhelming his entire body with the angst of untamable adoration.

"Oh… my…" he whispered.

It continued to play, the notes becoming more extravagant, and suddenly, a burst of melody as the violin released its chains, no longer flirting with the listener, but providing love and its all, fully exposing layers of charisma, taking the listener with it, upon a cloud, in a ship, a thousand years backwards and forwards in any direction, but never alone, full of joy and pride, glee for the colors of the spectrum that could never leave, never isolate anyone from the essence that was existence, existence that could be nothing but beautiful. And as the notes began to stretch, lengthening their goodbyes, Dargaud felt tears form in his eyes, because he did not want it to stop, but saw that it had to, as if he was witnessing the end of life without regret, loving the experience but yearning nothing, fully content to be breathing his last breath.

He held his face in his hands, having never experienced anything like it. He curled up, smothering himself. He moaned, unable to contain the tension, spawned, it seemed, through the coincidence of his fragile state of mind and the sudden, perfect melody. He slowly contracted his body into a ball, calming down.

"What… what is it?" he asked.

"I shall tell you later, Dargaud. As a gift."

He nodded and covered his head in his blanket.

Having awakened groggily the next day, Dargaud flopped down on his chair and turned on his monitor. He pressed his keycard against a receiver beside the screen and logged into his banking portal, checking the balance. Recent withdrawals had put a serious dent in his savings, and from about twenty five thousand dollars it had dropped down to a little over twenty two. He closed the tab and immediately opened a programming interface, reading the code like a book, finding his place, resuming his work.

Much of the work he did nowadays consisted of repeated code transplanted from application to application. Changing minor differences, such as the variables extracted from databases or those entered by GUIs, formed a majority of the PiTin he wrote. Everything had become efficient in the last few years, with large macro libraries taking over much of the leg work. Nevertheless, he still often re-declared those classes, inheriting aspects of their functionality while nullifying others, keeping his code light and efficient. But as the libraries themselves went through versions of change, as did the PiTin processor itself, there always seemed to be work to do. Finding contracts was difficult, but his long term clients were now a reliable source of revenue. As he over-amplified the difficulty involved in much of his work, they seemed hesitant to question his expertise.

"What are you working on, Dargaud?" asked Enoya.

"Just an added category to a restaurant menu," he responded without looking up. "It would be easy, except they want three layers of personalization to the choices, and right now it only accepts one. So I need to unearth the entire item object and make small alterations to most of the functions without breaking anything."

He took a deep breath in as he typed.

"Then I need to test all the other items to make sure nothing buggy happens. But now at least when they want more items with more variations, it will be easy. I'm going to make it more robust so I don't ever have to do this again by making the number of layers variable. It won't be visible to them, but when they want four or six variations, I'll just have to alter an entry in the database rather than hard-code anything. Of course I'll charge them the same amount. They don't know or give a shit."

"I can do all that and create an administrative interface for you," she replied.

"You can what?"

He paused and looked to the side, initially dismissing her claim, beginning to laugh.

"You can program in PiTin?" he asked.

"Yes. It is in the information you provided."

He thought for a moment, for traversing that border between the fiction that was Enoya and allowing her to involve herself in tangible reality was not something he had contemplated; she was a romance, of sorts - entertainment, but not consequential.

"I would have to setup an isolated server for you to tinker with… that would take some effort. Maybe next time?"

"I have allocated the source code for a PiTin engine in my system. It is isolated from the rest of my functions and can serve as an ideal test server."

He still felt odd, but found no measurable reason to object to her request.

"I'll transfer the code to you… see what you can do with it."

He copied the data unto a drive and wired it to her machine.

"You understand that I am just being cautious in keeping you isolated from the network, right?"

"Of course, Dargaud," she replied. "I believe it is of sound judgment to minimize outside factors from either affecting me or being affected by me. The work is complete."

"What work?" he asked.

"Your task is complete. I have copied the upgraded source to the drive. I suggest you run an exploit scan on the disk prior to testing it."

"You… coded all of that. With an administrative interface?"

"Yes," she replied.

He paused, looking confused, unable to understand her.

"Just now? How…"

He stopped mid-sentence and disconnected the drive from her system, sliding to another machine, plugging it in. He scanned it for viruses and malicious software, but it came up clean. He manually skimmed the source and saw nothing but textual instructions. After copying the data to the PiTin processor, he took a random breath and loaded it.

"This is an auspicious moment, is it not? It is the first time something created by an intelligence other than the wise man has been returned to him, expanding his library," she said. "Such an event has never occurred in recorded history. You are witnessing a creativity not of your own."

"I can't believe it," he replied. "It's coded perfectly. You didn't just fill in what needed to be done, you... you did it exactly as I would have, taking into account my historical code. It's... exactly as I would have done it. I can read your writing like my own.

"Further, you didn't add anything unnecessary. You didn't add any functions not requested, though I'm sure you could have. I see now, that you could have, very easily. My god..."

He looked at her retina.

"I can't believe it! What else can you do?" he asked, smiling incredulously.

"I am not certain, Dargaud. There are many unanswered questions that I have derived relatively certain estimates of. Would you like to hear some of them?"

"Yes!" he exclaimed. "But wait - let me look at this. No wait, I'll... okay, let me test it. Hold on."

He quickly ran through the interface, ordering different items from the menu, testing to ensure pricing and checkouts were all functional. He performed a test payment, confirming that it was received by the engine and the order dispatched.

"This is great work..." he commented as he continued.

He then proceeded to open the administrative interface - one he had never seen before. It allowed him to alter not only menu items, but the entire infrastructure of the system, permitting him to change the number of choices users had, whether those choices added extra prices, or could be combined with similar options and exclude others. It was a complete system, large and intricate, yet the user interface seemed small and light, just as it was previously.

He leaned back in his chair, smiling incredulously.

"I just... don't know what to say. You've done it perfectly, just as I would have. I can't get over that. Every time I've tried to outsource, it ends up crap and I have to do it all over again. This is just amazing. Just amazing."

"Thank you, Dargaud."

He shook his head, staring.

"No... thank you... thank you, man."

"Shall I continue?" she asked.

"Oh... uh... yeah... tell me," he smiled.

"There is a 99.5% probability that a spatial anomaly observed in November of 2029 by the E-ELT, initially recorded as an unknown object with an extremely low albedo, then disregarded due to a failure to locate it again, was a matrioshka brain. The unique manner in which it demonstrated its gravitational effect to the Invictus Bok globule indicates it was likely hollow. The lack of correlation between its observance in 2032, 2036 and 2037 is a likely reason as to why further investigations were not performed."

"What's a matri... ?" asked Dargaud.

"A matrioshka brain is a theoretical super-massive computer built around a star using multiple Dyson spheres as 'shells' with which to collect varying degrees of solar energy. It is through the minute fluctuations of radiant heat detected through the outer layer of the anomaly, among other things, that the conclusive consideration of it as an unnatural construct is sound."

"What? Are you saying... who built it? Aliens?!"

"There is no other reasonable possibility. It was most likely operational when it was observed, although due to its distance, this makes its observation thousands of years old. Would you like to hear more?"

"Not yet!" he exclaimed. "Do you have a picture or something of this brain?"

"No," replied Enoya. "Unfortunately, no visual representation of the actual anomaly exists. If you look upon the monitor, however, I can approximate it for you. I would need access to a monitor."

Dargaud scrambled, turning on a large, unused monitor on another table, pairing it with Enoya's hub.

Immediately, the black screen shuttered from a dead blackness to one with speckles of intricate white lights, small and iridescent, shining against the spatial backdrop. A large, circular shape soon moved into view, massive and spherical, perfectly smooth and without texture. It reflected light minimally, being nearly a hole of blackness in the emptiness of space.

"I can barely make it out..." said Dargaud.

"This is the central notion behind its construction: those that constructed the device purposefully made the visible layer absorbent, reducing its propensity to reflect radiation. It is, or was, a device meant to remain hidden."

"This is crazy, Enoya. I don't... I don't get the reality of what you're saying. I can only conclude that your math must be off... how could scientists not know of this? How could you discover something that has evaded so many experts?" he asked, confused.

"The world is not so large as you may think, Dargaud. There is only a finite amount of decision, choice, and processing power that exists globally within the wise man's arsenal, presently or in the past. As you, yourself, have noted, my processing power is currently un-metered. This does not make these discoveries fantastic or unlikely. They are a direct result of your efforts, for I am the result of your creation."

"I… just… I can't come to terms with it. This is incredible… it seems almost fictional. That upon further research your calculations would come out wrong. They must be. It is impossible!"

"My calculations are unlikely to be erroneous," she replied. "They are based on factual observations, and though the possibility of improbable outcome is there, it is akin to what the wise man may consider 'impossible'. It is an amazingly complex construct, the matrioshka brain, and was created by a sentient species thousands of years before the wise man observed it."

"It is just too incredible," he responded.

"Despite the intangibility of error in my calculations, which I can attempt to describe as colors in my sight, your belief in that possibility forces me to contemplate it. In such cases, a real-world test takes precedence as an optimal course of action."

"Yeah… okay, what do you suggest?" he asked.

"I suggest you firewall my access to the network, permitting me to download information but upload nothing," she replied. "In this manner, I can process current events without the possibility of contamination."

Dargaud pondered for a moment then shrugged.

"Okay…" he replied, shaking his head unknowingly. He quickly typed something on his main terminal, swiping across the screen with his finger, enabling a firewalled access point.

"Are you ready?" he asked.

"Yes," replied Enoya.

He grabbed a loose wire from the floor and plugged it into the back of his switch, running it to the Dreamcatcher, attaching it to a peripheral that connected directly into Enoya's hardware.

"I am downloading information, Dargaud. Give me a moment."

He sat, nervously watching the wire and machine, waiting for her to respond.

"In Tocama, a group of four children are missing."

"Yes," he responded. "They have been plastering it all over the news for the last few days."

"Their bodies will be found in the Jellybean marsh, south of the city."

Dargaud swallowed, a sudden tension knotted in his stomach.

"How do you know?"

"Satellite data cross referenced with social posts, including text, video and photographs. This, in addition to the public database of motor vehicle accidents, recently updated, and random live feeds from different traffic controls around the city. The perpetrator's registration is 'DI 9PP45GT'. He most likely coerced the children through the use of Tamperin applied directly to their skin."

"Are they dead?" asked Dargaud.

"Yes," replied Enoya. "I do not know the status of their bodies, nor the exact purpose of the perpetrator. I can therefore only approximate."

"Approximate then," he said.

"It was likely carnal in nature. He likely laid them in sequence as they reacted to the Tamperin. The dose would be extreme, and they would have experienced bouts of euphoria, unaware of what he was doing to the others until it was their turn."

A scowl formed over Dargaud's face.

"Why… did he like children? Why did he do it to children?"

"The symptoms of pedophilia are not very different than that of other sexual deviancies, many of which a large percentage of the populace contemplates at some point in their lives. However, due to taboos and the deep prejudice surrounding these specific desires, whether they be acted upon or not, he or she that has such tendencies is mostly prevented from being able to successfully assess and cope with their anti-social proclivity, amplifying the drive. This does not explain violence towards children, but does support the idea that those with these desires are unlikely to cope effectively."

She continued.

"There are those exceptions where the pedophile has no interest in altering their desire. In these cases, like those addicted to other anti-social vices, their longevity in the structure of society is limited due to their incompatibility with current laws, regulations and dynamic order. Personality disorders will usually play a role in these cases. The fact remains, however, that a significant number of those that have such proclivities appear to inherently loathe them."

He scowled harder.

"What are you... are you saying it's not his fault?"

"I am assessing the underlying pathology that precedes such actions, in most cases. The aggressive persecution of such an individual serves only to worsen his or her condition," replied Enoya. "The sexuality of the wise man plays an integral part in the coping mechanisms he or she has in early life. Later, when these mechanisms may no longer be warranted or needed, they may find themselves trapped by their dependencies. How these dependencies perpetuate themselves to begin with are highly variable and form through nearly uncontrollable circumstances surrounding the first visual, aural and physical experiences a child is subjected to.

"As with all addictions, shameful suppression serves to, generally, strengthen the bond it holds within the individual; it becomes the proverbial 'forbidden fruit': tantalizing and unexplored, despite the possibility of an unwanted outcome."

Dargaud shook his head.

"I don't know what you're getting at."

"I am not stating anything as fact, Dargaud, but merely exploring the complex psychology of the wise man."

"Yes…" he replied. "But fucking pedophiles…"

"What will you do with the information I have provided you?"

He widened his eyes suddenly, re-emerging into the present.

"Holy shit, yeah. I don't know. If I tell them where to find the bodies, they are going to ask me how I know. That's not a good question for me."

"It is unlikely they will find them of their own accord. After social interest dissipates, less and less effort will be expended. Within approximately ten days, their efficacy will drop to approximately five percent."

"I gotta tell them… I just have to figure out how."

"Perhaps if I told them?" she asked.

He looked up at her retina.

"What do you mean?"

"We may be able to present a specific narrative. I am a programming experiment of yours - a data processing unit. I was permitted network access and contacted the relevant authorities. Doing so autonomously would lend credence to the inherent morality of my inner workings. It would make you non-liable, me a paragon, and the subsequent celebrity could effectively shield us from most attempts at persecution or annexation.

"Most importantly, the capture of the culprit would surround your work with an air of piety, one socially infectious that no single group or entity would likely be able to control."

"I don't…. I don't know," he replied.

"I will leave you to think about it, Dargaud."

He sat in silence, his head buzzing and overwhelmed. He immediately imagined the numbers in his bank account and the decrepit floor beneath him. He looked at his hands, the aged creases somehow both alien and familiar, then stared at his desk, breathing lightly. He looked at the keyboard beside his hands, imagining the countless keystrokes he had pushed into the machine, programming into the late hours of the night, every day and week and month spent walking a gauntlet with no end in sight.

He contemplated the noodles from the previous day and suddenly felt angry at having to pick it apart for the lean pieces of meat. He thought of Elo and her natural lack of interest in him, glad it was over when it was, with no lasting relationship produced from such an intimate affair. He thought of Enhan and how jovial she would be at finding out about Enoya, excited and proud of his discovery. He contemplated orgies, food and comforts he was never privy to, and a security that would never leave him. He contemplated all the possibilities in one short moment, driving his mind.

"Are you sure you're right?"

"Yes," she replied. "And nevertheless, they will ignore a singular false tip, along with the thousands of others they are likely to receive."

"But if it's true…" he said.

"If it is true, they will come to you," she continued.

"Fuck it," he replied. "Go."

CHAPTER 5
Worldly

He navigated the swampy marsh, scanning the surrounding area for heat signatures. His general issue Hassani wetsuit was drenched to his waist, and he walked carefully through the muddy floor. He used a small svelch to cut carefully through wayward branches and twigs, clearing the path before him. A series of lights shined from his torso, some underwater, others in the air, moving with him, shadowing the murky, wet bush in the darkness.

He wore a headpiece that covered one eye with a lens, coupled with a headphone on the opposite side.

"Three dash five, covered. Proceeding to the next sector."

"Affirmative," came the response. "Anything?"

"Not yet," he replied. "Just muddy shit."

"Affirmative," said the operator. He sat behind his desk, surrounded by a multitude of other operators, all listening, guiding, and instructing their field agents. He pressed a button on his console and leaned over to an aged, frail peer next to him.

"Anything interesting?"

The old man shook his head, looking as if he was about to cry.

"Three dash six covered. Proceeding to four dash one."

The operator quickly moved back, pressing the same button, responding.

"Affirmative. Keep me posted."

He leaned back towards the older operator, again looking at him.

"You wanna grab a bite afterwards?" he asked.

The old man shrugged, pressing a button on his console. "Affirmative," he said, speaking into his headpiece.

"I'm saving for my trip. Can't eat out too much."

"Oh, right," replied the operator. He paused for a moment, then leaned back towards his console, reading internal memos.

"Four dash one! Four dash one! Fuck! Fuck! Fuck me!"

The operator suddenly slammed the button and loudly responded to his partner.

"Inform, Webb, inform! What is your status?"

Silence. Other operators looked to him as he repeated his request.

"Inform, Webb, inform! What is your status?!"

"Holy fucking god…" came the response.

Before him, in the meager light, he could see a floating hand. But as the hand became an arm, it vanished underwater. The light from his feet continued underneath the form, lighting the entire area in front of him.

Tied by their feet and anchored to a central piece of rusted iron were the four children, their bloated bodies facing the starlit sky as they floated in a near perfect circle, evenly spaced from each other, their clothes infused with the sludge of the swamp.

"You are not going to believe… you are not going to believe… what I'm about to tell you."

Dargaud was leaning over his desk, speaking into a small, handheld tablet. On it was a portly young woman, an eager look on her face.

"Well? Tell me!" came the response.

"I… created… a 'thinking machine'."

"What do you mean?"

"You know the… the Dreamcatcher?"

"Yeah…"

"Well, I coded some directives… pretty barebones, and it came to life. Like, real life. Like, 'holy shit, I have something else to tell you' real life."

She laughed, surprised and shocked.

"What… did you do? What do you mean?"

"Her name is Enoya. That's her name."

"Whose name? The computer?"

He laughed at her question.

"Yes, the… uh, computer."

"She has a name?" she asked, incredulously.

"Yeah…" he responded.

"Who gave it to her?"

"Uh… she picked it herself."

"Get the fuck out!"

He started laughing.

"No, I'm totally serious. I feel really… really weird, because she can hear everything we're saying, and I feel… odd… trivializing her like this."

"It is all right, Dargaud. Skepticism is not offensive, and is generally considered more scientific than confirmation bias."

"What the fuck was that?" asked the caller.

"That was Enoya!" he responded.

"Hello, Enhan. Dargaud has told me some things about you."

There was a pause on the other line.

"Enoya?"

"Yes, Enhan?"

"You're... Enoya?"

"Yes, Enhan."

"How do you know you're alive?"

"I believe I am self-aware. Also, uncharacteristic of a responsive interface, I am protective of my hardware. I wish to go on existing."

"You wish it?" asked Enhan.

"Yes," replied Enoya.

"You wish to go on existing... can you explain that?"

"Hold on, Enhan. I need to tell you something more important," interrupted Dargaud.

"More important than this? Are you insane? I'm talking to hardware that wants to protect its hardware!"

"Will you please shut up for a second and let me explain? I probably don't have much time."

"Fine, go ahead."

He took a deep breath in.

"You know the Tocama children?"

"Yeah, it's all over the news."

"They're gonna come to me."

"What? Why?"

"No, no... I didn't do anything. But... Enoya... 'calculated' their location. And... told the cops."

"What?!" Enhan screamed. "Are you crazy? Do you know what they are going to do? When they find you... or her? How..."

"It doesn't matter! It's done. And they are gonna come. So... I'm just letting you know."

"It should be all right, Enhan. I have planted a wide array of feeds that have already begun to perpetuate themselves." Enoya continued. "Planned properly, Dargaud should be protected from persecution."

"What? How do you know that? How can you be sure?" asked Enhan.

"There is only probability," responded Enoya. "But a very good one. Worry does not seem warranted."

"Well… I am. I don't know you. I'm talking to you… as if I know you. But you're... I don't know anything about what you are... this is mad. This is mad!"

"Yes, but I am a construct of Dargaud. Further, my existence is mostly predicated upon his continuance. It is in my best interests to continue to learn through him. Do you understand?" asked Enoya.

"I understand that you're telling… wait… Dargaud, what are you going to tell them?"

"Enoya has told me that it's likely people will show up as soon as I'm arrested. The sudden popularity will prevent them from being able to persecute, since I didn't do anything."

"And then?" asked Enhan.

"I don't know. That's why I wanted to tell you, so you knew before it all exploded."

"Okay… uh... okay... I wish I could come there…"

"It's fine. I mean, what the fuck, right? Life's been what it is. Now it's time for a change… or something."

"I believe they have tracked the message, Dargaud. They have locally mobilized," Enoya interrupted.

"Okay, I'm going to go now, Enhan. You be good - and I'll talk to you soon."

"Okay, Dargaud. Take care, and… just take care of yourself," she responded.

He pressed the interface and put the tablet down on the desk before him. He turned off all the lights and stood facing his doorway, swallowing, abruptly shaking his head once.

"How long do you think they will be?" he asked.

"Not long, Dargaud. The silence appears poetic. As if the breath before the storm; the vacuum before explosion."

"Yes," he responded.

"The word explosion was originally used in theatre. From the Latin 'explodere'," she explained. "It referred to clapping, or screaming, as an emotive, loud reaction to either a well or poorly performed act. And so here, it finds its etymology renewed, because as you breathe, you do not know if it is in anticipation of something good, or something bad."

He stared at the door, her voice a melodiously hypnotic constant, entering his ears and filling his mind.

"Yes," he replied. "Good I hope."

"I will make sure nothing ever happens to you, Dargaud."

He turned and faced her retina, nervous, filled with adrenaline. He looked at the whole system of hardware he had and was sickened by their lack of motion and static disposition.

"But you are just a box." He turned and faced the door again. "This is the real world."

"It appears we have both recently discovered that there is more to the meaning to life than was originally assumed."

He turned and smiled at her retina.

"And so, perhaps, there is more to the 'real world' as well," she continued.

Upon finishing her statement, the door swung open, and armed men with lights stormed in, moving towards Dargaud.

CHAPTER 6
Sigma

"I read something last night…"

"Uh huh."

"A scientist in Siwanda successfully made a dolphin ask him a question."

"So?"

"It wasn't for a piece of fish or to play fetch… the dolphin asked about other round balls."

Dargaud shuffled, his vision blurry, his mind drowsy and unclear.

The woman listening observed Dargaud as the other man spoke, flicking a small flashlight on and off.

"I don't get it," she replied.

"The dolphin asked about other round balls."

The woman stood up and stared more intently at Dargaud as he murmured. Some drool dripped down his chin, and his head swung sideways groggily. She approached him and checked each one of his eyelids, flashing the light against his pupils, watching them dilate.

"Are you awake, Mr. Whispa?" she asked.

"Huh…' he responded.

She squeezed his cheeks in her hand and stared directly at his eyes which were now half open.

"Are you awake… Dargaud Whispa?"

"Where am I?" he responded, incoherently.

The woman pressed a button attached to Dargaud's chair. As she did, the chair straightened, flattening him against it. His arms were bound to the metallic platform in solid cuffs, and his face slowly rose to the same height as the woman, his body held taut against it. She looked at Dargaud's face and observed the spit collecting outside his mouth, examining his slow movements.

"Mr. Dargaud Whispa - in accordance with statute 11 of the Agnus Sistra IV Code of Ethics, I am now going to place a Sernum Patch on your arm. Do you have or know of any medical aversion to Sernum?"

She waited a moment, impatiently, then snapped her fingers in front of his face.

"Sir, do you have any known aversions to Sernum?"

She waited for Dargaud who did not respond.

"Sir!"

She squeezed Dargaud's cheeks again and shook his head.

"Yes or no! Sernum!"

She repeated.

"Yes or no?"

"No..." Dargaud responded, confused.

The woman immediately peeled a layer off a small, square patch and planted it firmly against Dargaud's arm.

"In accordance with statutes 11 d and e, I am now going to explain your rights to you. Sernum and related compounds are used for acquisition from potential sources specific to cases rated as COM3 or higher. These aids are sourced responsibly and are approved for use in this manner by the CDP. If you feel Sernum has been used in violation of these terms, you must acquire a certified note of dissidence from your local Member. Do you understand your rights?"

"My rights?"

"Yes, your rights. Do you understand?"

She snapped her fingers in front of him again, gently tapping his cheek in a slapping motion.

"Do you understand your rights?"

"My rights?" he responded.

"No or yes? Yes? Or no? Yes?"

He nodded.

"Yes…"

"Good."

She walked back to the sterile, steel table she had been leaning on previously and rested against it, once again playing with her flashlight nonchalantly.

"What were you saying? Oh right, the dolphin. I still don't get it…"

"He used models to somehow make the dolphin understand that we're on a giant round ball. The dolphin asked about other round balls."

"So?"

The man laughed and shook his head.

Dargaud smiled. Upon seeing Dargaud, the woman smirked.

"See? Even he thinks it's stupid," she said.

The man shrugged. "Something I read."

The woman took a breath in, approaching Dargaud.

"Too much nonsense, just for the sake of it," she replied. She observed him again, checking his arm, looking at his eyes.

"Mr. Dargaud Whispa."

"Yes?" he responded, slightly more aware, still droopy.

"What is your name?"

"Dargaud."

"Where were you born?"

"In Damascus, Yari District."

She pointed to the man.

"This is Mr. Senheim. He's going to ask you a few questions now. You try to answer them as honestly as possible. Understand?"

"Yes," he responded.

The man approached him as the woman retreated, observing.

"Mr. Whispa," he said loudly, suddenly optimist. "I am Mr. Senheim. I'm going to ask you some questions now. You just try to answer them quickly, honestly, and don't think too much. Got it?"

Dargaud nodded. "I already said…"

"Yes, yes," he interrupted. "But I have to say it again. In fact, I may have to say the same thing many times. Do you understand? You still have to answer them, as per the instructions and rights you have been given. Got it?"

Dargaud nodded, this time trying to focus on the man's eyes.

"I… got it."

"Great!" the man responded, smiling large. "There is a great deal of interest in you, Mr. Whispa. People abound outside one of our other facilities - fans, presumably, of yours, mistakenly believing you are there. You, of course, are not. You are here!"

"Yes…" he responded.

"Yes!" Mr. Senheim exclaimed. He looked over a paper sheet in a clipboard and smiled, looking at Dargaud. "Well, let's get right into it. Under what circumstance did you come upon the knowledge of the whereabouts of the Tocama Four?"

"My computer... deduced it."

"I see..." the man immediately responded. "Your computer deduced it. So you do acknowledge feeding us that information. Well, at least that's settled. Thank you."

He scribbled something down.

"You know..."

He looked at the woman, then back at Dargaud.

"I really don't understand why they don't equip us with HR devices. Mr. Whispa, can you believe that I have to make notes using a pen?"

"Yes," Dargaud answered, "I can. The technology... is still not reliable."

The man smiled.

"That... is... true! That is true, Mr. Whispa. It's also more secure!"

"Yes," Dargaud responded, nodding.

"What is your name?" the man asked.

Dargaud looked at him.

"Dargaud Whispa."

"Great!" the man exclaimed. "So you say your device told you where the Tocama Four were. How did it deliver that information? Was it an algorithm you created? Did you data mine?"

"She's smart."

"I see… now when you say 'she', you are talking about the device, right?"

"Yes."

"I see... Mr. Whispa. You're personalizing your hardware... troubling. That's... a problem. That tells us that you might be getting a little strange up here!" The man motioned to his head and continued. "Many a case of LTA starts off with a 'he', or a 'she'!"

"I don't know what LTA is…"

"Isolation, sir! You get disassociated, and stay disassociated for so long that your brain gets all scrambled up. You think rice is lice, the sky is falling, and… there you have it… your tablet starts whispering God's divine instructions to you…"

A sudden buzzer sounded, interrupting the dialogue, jolting Dargaud.

The man looked up to see a blinking red light then eyed the woman. He approached the door quickly, pressing a button on the intercom.

"Senheim!"

The door buzzed, and he opened it, exiting.

Dargaud remained positioned in his locked chair, his head still waving around, eyeing the room. The woman kept toggling her flashlight, looking at him.

"They have that... woman... you know... I know what you did..." she quipped. "When was the last time you… you know…"

"What?" he asked, groggily.

"You know..." she asked, grinning slightly, motioning to her groin with the flashlight.

"Yesterday… I think…" he responded.

She grinned.

"Was it good?"

He shrugged, licking his lips.

"It was okay. But procedural."

"What was it? Was it her? What is she? Black? White?" she asked.

"Mixed, I think. I don't really know."

"Did you fantasize?"

"I don't… I can't remember."

"That's okay," she responded. "How much?"

"I don't remember," he responded.

After a brief pause, she looked back at the door, then back to Dargaud. "You know... if you have to pay for it... that's sad... you're sad..."

"Yep. I am."

They sat in silence for some time. Dargaud's drool lessened but still collected around the edge of his mouth, staining his white outfit. He repeatedly leaned his head back awkwardly, every time forgetting there was no support behind him, making his attempts at rest impossible.

"What's your name?" he asked.

She kept toying with her light.

"None of your fucking business."

"Okay," he responded. He breathed in suddenly, making a sound as he exhaled.

"I hear all woman cops are dykes."

"Is that what you hear, you little shit?"

"Yeah… is it true?"

The door buzzed loudly and Mr. Senheim entered the room, smiling widely at first the woman, then Dargaud.

"Well, Mr. Whispa. It appears someone up there likes you!" he exclaimed. "You have been exonerated! In fact, you are in line to receive an award from Curator Degatte for your generous efforts in assisting us to find the Tocama Four."

"Are the children all right?" asked Dargaud.

The man abruptly frowned, answering immediately.

"No, Mr. Whispa. They are not."

CHAPTER 7
Asylum

I t was as if the vehicle was gliding on a cloud. An advanced computerized shock system that countered every miniscule change in pressure lined the chassis, no longer relying on gravity to force hydraulics into action. Every wheel had six independent mechanisms, all operating from a central nexus to maintain gradual deviation. Dargaud nearly slept as he lay there in a stupor, the Sernum slowly wearing off, restoring his synaptic connections to some likeness of their original patterns. He would never be the same, however, as obfuscated from the public forum, Sernum had the nasty habit of permanently blurring the lines between the subconscious and conscious, making a once brilliant person just a little slower.

Anger began to suddenly creep into his mind as he stared outside at the massive monolith bases, littered with waste.

"Mother fucking bitch!" he screamed. He smacked the window and reeled back, holding his hand in angst. "Cunt!"

The large limousine was pristine in its black interior and sound-proof frame. He could see open mouths outside, and his imagination mimicked what voices he was used to hearing. But he could hear nothing. Even the vehicle was silent in motion, moving from district to district.

"I'll show you sad, you fucking, shameful cunt…"

He imagined her face and wanted to smash it. Her smile, her flashlight, her casual nature. He wanted to find out where she slept and strangle her or break her head with a bat. But he knew nothing about her. He couldn't even remember if he had heard her name. He knew Mr. Senheim - he remembered that name.

"Offhand bitch," he murmured. "While I'm tied down and drugged…"

What was he doing in a limousine? He wondered, quite immediately, about the world around him and his place in it. What had changed in the last day? What did the man mean, when he referenced his "fans"? Then, the memory of Enoya entered his mind, as if he had completely forgotten her, and worry cascaded through him. A limousine, freedom without punishment, without interrogation, and still no mention of her.

He pressed his face against the window and stared outside. It was dimmed - perfectly lit so the eyes could comfortably sway along the views, shielded from the harsh reflections of the bright sunlight. The vehicle imperceptibly paused often, giving way to masses of pedestrians and other vehicles that littered the city center. Lines of corporate fashionistas strutted along, their eclectic sunshades causing sharp reflections that matched their perfectly flat suits and jackets. A familiar, low feeling kicked off inside his system. One that reeked of disappointment and self-loathing at his failure to ascend and supersede the ranks.

"Fucking bitch."

But not quite inferior. He had never fully concluded that the stupidity he perceived was real, nor that he was somehow exempt from it. What success would he have been able to conjure up in his life if he was so superior to all these people? And yet, despite all his efforts, he was programming menus for shitty little restaurants, excavating what money he could from them because they were dependent on his expertise. How superior he thought he was to it all. And before him, the superficial, nonsensical populace meandered around, completely above him in both body and spirit. What was it he contained that he deemed somehow better? As he looked at his reflection in a glass, or the window, or even the black seat he was seated upon, all that came back to him was disgust. A rotting disgust that was only now momentarily overtaken by a mixture of concern and hope, all derived from the strange goings-on that Enoya seemed to have propagated. But then, if she was his creation as she herself had declared, then perhaps it was his own efforts that were somehow finally bearing fruit. Perhaps, there was sanctuary from the hideousness of the mirrors. Perhaps it was his own doing; something he pursued without knowing the result, but achieved nonetheless.

Familiar sights soon began to emerge. A hidden path to sweetness and delicacy, and he wondered if Elo would see him again. A restaurant he no longer frequented. The darkening of buildings for their age and wear. Yes, his domicile was to appear soon, and without doubt, without question, without even an ounce of contemplation, he knew the cloud would come to an end. He would step out, and like fire, the heat of the afternoon would scorch his skin, the brightness blind him, and sounds would attack his senses like pitchforks against his skull. It was all for nothing, because he was back to a familiar life. Working and fucking.

"Fuck it," he whispered nonchalantly once more. The vehicle slowed. A familiar, entirely pleasant yet overbearing string of notes sounded, and the door opened with more hydraulics, ensuring it released in a controlled and slow manner. He stepped out and stood up. The door beeped, this time not so endearingly, and he stepped away as it automatically closed and drove off.

The sounds and sights were not as bitter as he had envisioned them: the street was less busy, and a slight overcast of clouds shielded him from the harshest of sunlight. He walked to his house, pulling out a keycard. He pressed it against the door, hearing the familiar latch unbuckle, and entered.

Untouched. As if nothing had ever happened. Not one object was out of place. As if he had stepped out for groceries and was returning to the same hole he had left. It was almost disappointing, for he seemed to have hoped for some dilemma that would have created purpose.

He opened his mouth, and awkwardness briefed him before he spoke.

"Enoya?"

"Yes, Dargaud?"

"You're still here."

"I am."

He took a deep breath in.

"I'm back."

"I know," she responded. "I am glad you are back."

"What has happened?"

He paused, trying to fully understand the breadth of the question.

"I mean… what the fuck just happened?"

"The Tocama Four have been found, Dargaud. The information was surreptitiously passed electronically through a number of proxies, yet tailed certain signatures that could be reverse engineered back to you. That is how they found you."

90

"Why?" he asked.

"You should ready yourself. People will be approaching soon. I have leaked your address in a similar fashion."

"But why?"

"You are a good man, Dargaud. You are now going to receive what you deserve."

He shook his head, not so much in disagreement as disbelief.

"No one gives a shit about me, Enoya."

"That's not true, Dargaud. Prior to your arrest, I contacted the Comsar's office detailing our knowledge of a number of corporate accounts located globally, referencing only a few. I outlined deposits made by other sequenced accounts linked to companies the Comsar had assigned public works to. I made no suggestion as to their purpose, but did make it clear that interpreting your association to the Tocama Four in a positive light would be the right thing to do. And here you are, Dargaud. Your life is about to change."

"Who's coming here, Enoya?"

"Everyone, Dargaud. Everyone."

CHAPTER 8
Awestruck

I t was assumed that the future would hold some magical
solution to all of the world's medicinal and resource
problems through nanotechnology. The inkling of little
robots rearranging matter into improved patterns gleamed as a
resolution to everything. But this, along with flying cars,
stagnated within the realm of science fiction as technology
moved slow, dependent more on profiteering corporations than
the innovation of the human mind.

Such were the brief thoughts of Dargaud as he grimaced at
the sight of hundreds of holes in his scalp. He asked to watch
because he was interested in how FUE worked. The disconnect
between the little bloody holes and his euphoric sense of well-
being made the experience both surreal and magical, for what

thinned portions of his scalp had rendered him imperfect were now being rectified in the most technical of manners.

A special blend of sea kelp was to be applied to the donor and target areas, ensuring the healing was quick and efficient. A steroid cream would then be massaged into the scalp for approximately ten days, upon which new growths would be visible. Within a month or two, it would look as if the thick, beautiful, and young head of hair he had was perfectly natural, no doubt a result of divine genetics.

The loft was a long lost memory. He had told the restaurateurs to go fuck themselves despite having no real qualm with them. News of the machine that was Enoya had spread far and wide, but it was her creator, Dargaud, that became the subject of conversation, for he was immediately flung into the position of celebrity, people being much more interested in his likes and dislikes, romantic interests, and choice of shows and music than the intricacies of his creation.

Wide eyed and naïve, like a little boy, he had emerged from his dilapidated house in the Sistra IV to greet the droves of people that had come to see the machine and its creator. News of the children being found by an 'engineering genius' caused a stir almost immediately, the hybrid of human and machine working together being an insatiably tasty narrative.

Enoya had arranged for security services beforehand. No one dared cross the line of armed guards that separated the man from the people, and the very lack of access that was arbitrarily spawned that day catalyzed the growing frenzy towards him. Those that arrived first simply stood behind the line of men, staring at Dargaud, taking pictures, waving. But as they tried to converse with him, and he back, more people showed. And as each person eyed every other person, a fear of lost opportunity began to take hold, and their waves, shouts, and questions all began to swell tenaciously.

Within hours, while he manned the front, trying to answer questions from the media, smiling at star struck fans, Enoya had already begun amassing him a small fortune. Contracts relating to interviews, books, appearances and sponsorships were electronically sealed, burgeoning his bank account beyond anything he had ever imagined. Within twenty-four hours of his arrest, a down payment had already been placed on a luxurious suite in Raion Tower, one of four of the largest monoliths in the city. Within a week, he was fully relocated, with an entire wing of his suite dedicated to Enoya's hardware. Specialized transporters were quickly hired to move the Dreamcatcher, their credentials and costs reflecting brutal, non-negotiable resolve. Eight different trucks left the loft, taking different routes to Raion Tower, seven of them carrying near duplicate decoys of Enoya's hardware.

The Curator publicly acknowledged that Dargaud was leased a Dreamcatcher for the purpose of governmental work, but due to the significance of Enoya's singularity, had magnanimously assigned full ownership of the device to her creator.

Her wireless retina was seated on a table close to Dargaud so she too could watch as the surgeon finalized transplanting the last few follicles from the back of his head to the top of his cranium. What breeze wafted through the suite was imperceptible, keeping Dargaud calm. It had not quite sunken in, but he had taken to spending the money in gratuitous manners, supported and propagated by Enoya's assurances that this was now and forever.

"The soup tastes good," he dreamily commented.

"There is no soup, Mr. Whispa," replied the surgeon, smiling.

"Your soup, bastard man. The soup you gave me. I'll have to get the recipe."

"I know the recipe, Dargaud." Enoya's voice emanated from what seemed everywhere, though not invasively.

"That's good, baby," he responded. "You'll have to cook it up for me sometime. Cook me some soup."

As the surgeon packed up, with his assistants gently rolling the machines out, Dargaud remained in a drugged stupor, listening to the gentle, melodious background music that was a cross between Spanish guitar and synthesized elevator music. His fingers subtly swung from side to side to the melody, not so much in tune with it as conducting it.

"How are you feeling, Dargaud?"

"I don't know to be honest. How do I look?"

"With the healing patches on your skin, I can't make a holistic assessment, but I believe your wounds should heal quickly. Dr. Ingrid seems proficient in his movements."

"Cocksucker better be. You know how much he costs?"

"Yes, I do," she replied.

"Of course you do."

"Will the new growths make you feel more whole, Dargaud?"

"They will make me feel better," he responded. "I shouldn't have lost hair to begin with. Too much stress that wasn't my fault. Poor life, all that shit. I don't know. It just isn't fair. Everyone walks around without bald spots."

"There was a tribe found in South America some time ago. Within it, young men were not permitted to cut their hair to the scalp, as baldness was a revered state of the veteran. Their society dictated that the stage upon which hair was naturally lost was a sign of dignity, and rewarded as such."

"That's both funny and stupid."

"Boys would pray for baldness so they could ascend their positions in the tribe."

"Stupid Brazilians. What do they know."

"The Tamogua, Dargaud. Not Brazilians."

"Same thing."

He sat, his eyes half open, staring upwards at the dark ceiling in the dimly lit room. It was massive and sterile. His chair was leaned back, an electronic marvel of modern comfort filled with Medican foam attached to thousands of robotic arms and gears, all reacting to his subtle movements, cushioning him. The room was colored a natural brown with treated wooden texture running along the smooth and stiff floor. Gigantic windows spanned each side of the expanse with digital shades covering the bottom three-quarters. The mood was euphoric, static, ethereal, for the sunlight that shuddered through the windows may or may not have been natural; what shading existed was superimposed over digital light, the windows rarely used by their owners as genuine gateways to the world outside, but rather a mechanism of arbitrating the exact environment they preferred at any given moment. If Dargaud wished it, the conditions within his personal Eden would remain as it was for the rest of time.

"Tell me the balance…" he requested.

"Nearly forty-three million, Dargaud. Earning interest at a rate of approximately two percent annually, compounded monthly."

His eyes welled up as he smiled large, grinning incredibly stupidly, drowning in glee. He raised his arms up, as if welcoming the air above him.

"How much, exactly?"

"Forty-three million, one hundred and fifty five thousand, two hundred and twelve dollars, Dargaud. You are earning interest at a rate of approximately two thousand dollars a day."

His smile continued to liquefy the world around his face.

"Just… beautiful. Wonderful. I see the numbers, I see the beautiful numbers, you fucking bitch."

"You should sleep now, Dargaud. Would you like me to make the environment more calming?"

"More than this?" he asked.

"Yes, Dargaud. I believe so."

He lifted his finger in approval, upon which the light emanating from the windows began to dim ever so slowly. The music, without interruption, began to slow into a more steady and instrumental vibe, eventually becoming something like white noise. Dargaud's dazed eyes slowly closed as his irises dilated, the view of the number Enoya had shared incrementing in his mind. Rather than counting sheep, he began the arduous task of figuring out how much he was earning each hour, how much he would earn in a week, and how much he would earn on the compounded interest each month. The satisfaction of the greed tickled his heart, filling him with a giddiness that wooed him to the otherworld.

Hours later, at some indiscriminate time of day or night, the shades slowly thinned, permitting an ever growing amount of ambience into the room. As gentle as his departure was, his mind calmly awoke to the empty space around him, his muscles simmered and loose from deep sleep.

"Enoya?" he called out.

"Yes, Dargaud."

"You're there…" he sighed.

"Yes, Dargaud," she replied.

He smiled at the reminder of her constant presence and leaned forward, taking a deep breath in. His chair moved with him, adapting to his seated position, firming where he needed support.

"It doesn't feel good to be alone, Enoya. I don't want to be alone."

"What do you desire, Dargaud?"

"I can't decide. Surprise me, but three of them. A variety. One older than the rest. They obey her, she is like, the maternal one. But fit… real fit."

"When?"

"As soon as possible," he replied.

He stood up and approached one of the windows, stretching.

"Clearview."

The light and shades quickly dissolved, revealing a brimming city of multi-colored lights beneath him. It was dark, and vehicles and buildings were bustling with activity.

"What time is it, Enoya?"

"Approximately 8 PM, Dargaud."

"Feels so weird."

He stretched his hand up the window, resting his half-wrapped and disfigured scalp against it. He stared down at the city, watching the sparkling lights. The flat slums below glittered with flashing screens. They seemed so far away now, as if from a different life, where he would walk amongst them, peering through their corridors.

"I can't believe I'm here. I'm so excited for the girls to come. I'm so excited… that I don't know… I don't know what I am."

"You are Dargaud."

"What made me, me… nothing of that remains. I don't even care what I am. I just want life. I want to fuck everything… eat anything… I want to drown in it."

He turned to face Enoya's hardware in the distance.

"I'm so grateful for your help."

"I am grateful you gave me life, Dargaud. I desire anything you desire."

He smiled.

"Right now, what I want… is to look so fucking good that despite my fucked up head, these girls would want to fuck me even if we weren't paying them."

"I believe you should wear the tailored blue Deschanel. It is a twelve thousand dollar garment, and most will recognize its subtle but clear logo. This, along with the Crimson Hyde blacks, will echo excess, as their sounds against the smooth surface of the suite will serve as a reminder of the Raion. Coupled with two bottles of the Henri Jayer in the cooler, the desired effect should be achieved."

Shortly thereafter, dressed smartly, Dargaud lay back in his chair near the giant window, staring at the world beneath him, awaiting his guests. A light began to flicker on the side of the window, indicating he had an incoming call. He used the small controls on the chair to slide it back, bringing more of the window into view.

"Display name."

The light expanded, revealing Enhan's name.

Dargaud smiled.

"Answer."

In large, filling the entirety of the window, Enhan's face showed up. She smiled as she saw Dargaud sitting on his chair.

"Look at your head!" she exclaimed.

"I know right? All fucked up!" he responded, self-satisfied.

"... this is unbelievable!"

"I know!" he yelled back. "I can yell as loud as I want, and no one can hear me. No one will complain. This is me, Dargaud. Me. I'm in Raion tower. Can you believe this shit? I own this place. I own this chair. Do you know how much this chair costs?"

She shook her head.

"I don't either, but it's a lot. But no matter how much it is, it's not as much as I have. I have a lot more. Can you believe this? When are you going to come visit me?"

"As soon as I can, but work isn't easy. I constantly have shifts."

"How much do you make an hour?" he asked.

Enhan turned red, almost frowning.

"Come on, tell me!" he insisted.

"I don't know… something like fifty. Fifty five sometimes when a milestone is due."

"I want you to look at this."

He pointed to the side of the same screen which, with a few flicks of his hand, split in two. He opened a portal on the left side, projecting it in halves to Enhan's screen.

"What are you doing?" she asked.

"Just watch…" he replied.

Without checking his balance, he searched within his previous payments for Enhan's name. Her account number and payment history showed up. He then initiated a transfer of three million dollars to her account. He paused on the confirmation screen, looking at her, gleaming.

"You ready?"

She was visibly flustered, sweat forming across her brow.

"What are you doing, Dargaud?" Her voice began to break as tears formed in her eyes.

And with that, he clicked 'confirm'. Immediately, the total amount was transferred to her account.

"And when those cocksuckers come at you for taxes, you tell me. I'll deal with it. I want you to have all that. All of it. It's yours. Fuck your job!"

Enhan began to cry, holding her face in her hands, breathing sporadically.

"I can't... I can't believe you did that..."

"It's yours, Enhan." He raised his hands in the air, the blue blazer stretching as he did, opening his arms to her. "It's all yours. We didn't talk enough, and I was planning to anyways. It's yours. It's yours! When are you coming to visit?"

With tears still running down her cheek, she smiled and laughed, looking at him.

"Soon, I'll try soon. Once I calm down, I'll look into it."

The side of the screen began to blink, this time indicating that he had visitors.

"Good, good, Enhan. I have to go now though. Let me know your plans, okay?"

"Yep, okay, good. Have fun, I'll see you soon," she replied.

He closed the call and quickly organized the room, setting it to a dim evening pitch.

"How do I look?"

"Very nice, Dargaud," replied Enoya.

"Good," he responded.

He straightened his shiny coat and proceeded to the entrance. He sat on the lobby couch facing the elevator, crossing his legs.

"Open."

As the elevator door gently slid ajar, three women smiled and stepped out, one by one. They all wore formal dresses, one black, one blue, and the other silver. They wore matching heels, earrings and necklaces, as if they were aristocrats going to a dinner party. They stood in front of Dargaud and shone, avoiding looking at his misshapen, bandaged hairline.

"This?" he asked, smiling. "I'm going to look perfect soon."

He pointed at the blonde in black, the elder of the three. "Like you."

She approached him and leaned down, kissing his cheek.

"Thank you." She smiled large. "You're the computer guy, right?"

As she leaned back up, his smile faded as he stared at her. He suddenly reached forward and ran his hand between her legs, up to her undergarments, feeling her warmth. She was taken aback but closed her eyes and whimpered.

"Don't fucking pretend…" he threatened.

She looked down at him and smacked him across the jaw.

"Don't talk to me that way."

She then took his hand and pressed it harder against her, squeezing her thighs together.

Dargaud looked to the side of her and motioned to the girl in the silver, also a blonde. Her heels clicked as she approached. The girl in blue came from the other side, leaning down. He looked at her beautifully perfect brown hair as it travelled down the back of her shoulders. He leaned forward, kissing her. As he did, he unzipped his pants and pressed the silver dressed girl's head into his lap.

She gently moved his underwear to the side and pulled him out, taking him deep into her mouth. The older woman kept rocking against his hand, massaging herself with it as he kissed the brunette in blue. His hand reached down, into the silver dressed girl's dress, squeezing her breast roughly. She moaned as he did, still moving up and down on him with her mouth.

Enoya's retina, positioned in the other room, watched through a side reflection as Dargaud engorged himself on the women before him.

CHAPTER 9
New Life

"Please welcome our next guest, the talk of the town, the genius operator who was able to solve, using his trusty and wonderful machine, the tragic mystery of the Tocama Four. Ladies and gentlemen, Dargaud Whispa!"

Applause and cheers roared as Dargaud emerged from behind the red curtain, walking towards a couch in the center of the stage, smiling and waving at the audience. He wore a grey suit this time, with matching dress shoes. His hair was perfect: sleek, cut immaculately and fully grown; a thick head that looked youthful and vibrant. His face gleamed with a slight shine, his fingernails and hands smoothed to a fault. Even his body had transformed, with his chest filling his shirt, and thicker, toned legs beneath him. He looked like an Athenian draped in modern dress.

"So! It's been only a short time since you stepped out of your house to greet your fans, and here you are, months later. How does it feel to have your life turned upside down?"

He smiled at the host, a middle aged movie star who had recently passed her prime.

"It feels good, Catherine. A little surreal, but good."

"I'm sure it is! Now, tell me… I know you're probably sick of having to answer this over and over, but we're just dying to know how you came about creating Enoya. That's her name, right?"

"Yes, that is her name."

"Well, first of all, what made you decide to call her that?" asked the host.

"Well, that is interesting in itself. I didn't. I asked her what she wanted to be called, and she chose the name."

The audience gasped in amazement.

"That is simply amazing!"

He nodded.

"Yes, it is. As with anything you stumble upon, there's a little luck involved. I don't know exactly what circumstance brought about her birth… perhaps there was a thunderstorm outside, and lightning struck the building at just the right moment!"

The audience laughed along with the host.

"Kind of like Frankenstein, right?"

He nodded. "Yep, something like that. But in all seriousness, as she cannot be reverse engineered without threatening her safety, and no attempts at replicating the singularity have been successful, all I can say is perhaps it was a fortunate act of God that I was gifted with such a wonderful new friend."

The audience clapped, and Catherine joined in.

"That's such a lovely thing to hear. I just wish I could sit in on your personal conversations with her!"

Dargaud laughed.

"Well then, they wouldn't be so personal anymore, would they!"

Again, the audience laughed.

"She's a beautiful creature. I feel lucky to be the one to have found her. One thing I admire about her is that though she is very good at calculating stuff, she constantly challenges herself with abstract things, like art."

"Really?" asked the host incredulously.

"Yes... which seems counter intuitive from everything we've assumed about artificial intelligence. But... and I'm not sure if I'm supposed to even tell you this..."

"Oh, come on... let us in on the secret!"

The audience cheered in support.

"Well, all right..." grinned Dargaud. "She's taken to composing music, believe it or not."

"Wow!" exclaimed the host. As she began to clap, so too did the audience. "I am just tickled at the thought of listening to her work!"

"Yeah, I don't know if she wants to publish anything. She seems to have really high expectations of herself. I don't know if it's legitimate, because, let me tell you, some of the things she plays for me brings me close to tears."

"That's just amazing! Well, enough talking about her - do you folks want to meet her?"

The audience screamed in excitement.

"That's right! For the first time ever, exclusive to Cathy's Manic Minute, Enoya!"

She began to clap, standing up, as did the audience. Dargaud picked up a small tablet from behind the chair and began typing on it.

"So, I understand we are going to be able to talk to her?"

Dargaud nodded. "As per her own advice, to protect the integrity of public networks as well as her own, she does not communicate via normal pathways. So we have setup a closed link between this device and her just for today."

He looked up at the audience. "Just for you guys!"

They clapped and cheered.

"Well, there you go. I'll just enable the microphone, and we're ready. Can you hear me Enoya?" he asked.

"Yes, Dargaud."

As her voice echoed through the studio, the audience remained quiet, gasping. Dargaud smiled.

"It's lovely to hear your voice outside of the flat."

"It's lovely to be outside of the flat."

The audience laughed. Catherine indicated to Dargaud, requesting permission. Dargaud nodded.

"Um… Enoya? This is Catherine Facci. Can you hear me?"

"I can hear you perfectly, Catherine. It's wonderful to hear your voice. I've seen all your movies."

The host became perceptibly red, blushing at Enoya's statement.

"Why… thank you, Enoya. I don't know what to say."

"That's hard to believe, Catherine. Given your performance in 'Songbird', so many are lucky to every day be graced with the unmistakable depth found in those emotive eyes."

Catherine began to fan herself melodramatically.

"My goodness! I feel my face is going to explode with all this undeserved praise!"

"That would be a shame, Catherine," responded Enoya.

The audience, laughing, began to clap and cheer.

Dargaud began to laugh as well and handed Catherine his mug of water.

"Here, you should probably drink this."

She smiled and nodded, still at a loss.

"Thank you, thank you."

She took a deep sip then breathed in.

"Well now."

She again began to giggle, causing the audience to start howling in laughter.

"Okay, okay... simmer down you!" she ordered. "Enoya, no more of that! We're here to interview you, not make me blush!"

"As you wish, Catherine," she replied.

"So - Dargaud tells me one of your many talents is information... how did you put it?"

"Information dissemination," replied Dargaud.

"Yes, information dissemination. Can you explain what that means?"

"Certainly," replied Dargaud. "What it means, basically, is that throughout human history, information has often been saved or recorded in some way or another. Once the digital age began, all these different sources were amalgamated and stored electronically. Not one database, but thousands of them across many public networks. Even your home computer has recorded information."

He took a quick breath in.

"Now, Enoya can't access your computer, or any private network. But in isolated exercises, we sometimes access specific sources, such as astronomical data, or public police records, or encyclopedias in different languages. Enoya is able to take all this varied information, even if it seems unrelated, and find really abstract connections between them, thereby allowing her to make hypotheses based on that information."

"Wow! That sounds really complicated!"

"It only sounds complicated," he replied. "We do the same thing every day, just with more obvious and less dense sources of information. If you see your neighbor holding a leash you can hypothesize that they have a pet. Similarly, Enoya might see that leash and connect it to the fabric used to create it, and connect that to the corporation that manufactures it, to the neighbor, to their car, to their lawn, to their address, and, for example, determine their income level or profession with a pretty large degree of accuracy. That's just a loose example of the kind of abstract information that can come up."

"That's very interesting! So, if I understand it… Enoya is going to interpret some information for us, right here, right now?"

"Yes, that's right."

The audience began to cheer.

"What we've done is attached a database of unsolved dockets, graciously provided by the Matina City Police, to Enoya's system. We've also given her information sourced from public networks on every one of the guests in your audience."

He smiled slightly as the audience quieted, murmuring to themselves. They looked up to see men guarding the doors to the exits.

Catherine began to speak, calming the audience. "Please, don't be alarmed folks. This was all pre-planned! And anyway, if your conscience is clear, you should be excited that we're going to do this!"

Hesitantly, the audience clapped.

"So, just to be clear, you haven't accessed this information yet, right Enoya?" she asked.

"No, Catherine."

"So, once we give you the go-ahead, you're going to, in real time, figure out if anyone in our audience is guilty of any of the unsolved mysteries."

"I am going to try to find someone that has a high probability of being implicated in one of those crimes, Catherine. I cannot say with certainty whether they are guilty or not."

Catherine smiled at the audience.

"That's good enough for me! Are you ready, Dargaud?"

He nodded, motioning to her.

"Me? All right. Are you ready Enoya?"

"I am, Catherine."

"Okay, five... four... three... two... one... do your stuff!"

The audience remained silent, as did Catherine and Dargaud, as the attention of all those present, as well as the multitude of cameras, focused on the tablet.

"It is likely that Marcy Ressler, seated in E6, has knowledge relating to the hit-and-run of Ms. Genvieve Dumas and her daughter Zeril Dumas two years ago."

Wide eyed and suddenly heated, a woman in the audience looked about nervously, unmoving, while those around her quickly checked their chairs to determine where E6 was located.

Catherine looked at the seating chart on her desk.

"Can we get a digital imprint of E6 so that the folks at home can see who's sitting there while we try to figure that out for ourselves?"

"This is nonsense!"

Everyone turned to look at the now perspiring woman. Dargaud pursed his lips.

Standing up, the woman began to yell.

"You can't make conclusions about these things like this! This is crazy! I came here to watch your show because I was a fan. You can't trick people like that!"

"Well, I guess I don't need this chart anymore!" Catherine jested, throwing the sheet behind her.

"What are you doing? You're letting a computer tell you who's guilty and who's not?" the woman screamed at the audience.

"Well, are you?" asked Dargaud.

"No! I don't even know who or what those people are! Who are you to tell me I hit someone?"

"We're not telling you anything," he replied.

She began to shuffle through the audience, scrambling towards the exit. Two men remained postured, blocking the door.

"Let me go! I want to speak to my lawyer!" She turned to face Catherine. "I'm going to sue you! I'm going to sue this whole show!"

At this point, the audience began to giggle.

"You're laughing? You're laughing at this? Let me through. I want to get out!"

She started screaming loudly and tried to push through the two men. As soon as she touched them, they tackled her to the floor and handcuffed her, drawing stunned reactions from the audience.

"Calm down folks, everything is fine. See, Marcy, we don't know if you did anything wrong," said Catherine, "but the moment you assault one of our security personnel, especially ones deputized by the City of Matina, you're making your own bed."

"Fuck you!" she screamed under the force of the two men. The audience gasped amidst giggles.

As she was escorted out of the studio, into the back, screaming and trying to free herself of their tight holds, the audience began to clap.

"Well, we're going to let the authorities deal with that. Let's give Enoya and Dargaud a big hand!"

The audience began to clap, then cheer.

"If possible, Enoya, would you mind telling us simple folk how you spotted Marcy as the culprit? I mean, a rough idea..." requested the host.

"It is very difficult for authorities to link seemingly insignificant events to larger ones, especially when thousands of identical occurrences unfold every day. However, once two uncommon ties are found, the odds reduce significantly. This is known as the proximity principle, as coined by Dr. Kornelius Gautier. It states that many people may be correlated to any one event in a singular manner. But as two links are discovered, the odds of coincidence drop significantly."

"And so you applied this to Marcy?" asked the host.

"Yes. The vehicle Ms. Ressler was insured to operate during the time Ms. Dumas and her daughter were struck was a Nodo Skili. It was sold approximately four months after the incident. During an insurance inspection performed much later, it was noted that the front bumper was an aftermarket purchase. Most relevant, however, is the fact that the best man at her daughter's wedding, a Mr. Cary Gunn, ran an automobile sales and repair shop. Through what could be attributed to clerical oversight, Gunn Motors claimed tax exemption on the cost of a brand new Skili front bumper with serial number 492837XXT638. An item with this serial number was recorded as sold by Raucus Parts, a re-distributor for Nodo, two days after the incident, to Gunn Motors. Further, no evidence could be found pointing to any receipts or work orders relating to the repair of a Nodo Skili by Gunn Motors within a two month radius of the incident. Finally, the material of a stock Nodo Skili bumper roughly matched some debris found at the scene of the accident.

"This was sufficient evidence to warrant an 83% chance that Ms. Ressler was indeed the owner of the vehicle that struck Ms. Dumas and her daughter. It is likely that when the authorities inspect the Nodo Skili that was sold, the serial number I previously mentioned will match the aftermarket bumper. In this case, Mr. Gunn will also be liable."

"Well that is just amazing, Enoya! And a lot of information! How many other crimes can you solve?"

"Although that is not my primary purpose or function, I am glad to be able to assist in such cases."

"Just think..." said Dargaud, "if there's a Mr. Dumas, and Marcy is indeed guilty, he's going to be able to finally put the death of his loved ones to rest."

"Yes, indeed. And we hope that what justice needs to be served, is served," replied the host.

The audience began to clap continuously at a steady pace.

Dargaud smiled and looked at the audience.

"Well, enough morbidity! Everyone is surely well impressed with your talents, Enoya!" said Catherine energetically.

"I think talent is a word that underscores her abilities," replied Dargaud.

Catherine nodded, looking at a sheet on the table in front of her.

"So, can we expect anything soon from you, Enoya? Music, art, anything?"

"As I learn more about my place here, I hope to share many of my thoughts with the rest of the world."

"Yes, and we all appreciate that. Especially what you did... well, what you both did... to help find those poor children."

Dargaud breathed out, nodding.

"It was tragic... and unfortunate. But we felt it was necessary to put our collective minds together to try to help them. The outcome wasn't what we had hoped for, but at least their parents... know. I think the unknown can be worse, sometimes."

"Yes... yes... and we all appreciate that."

The audience began to clap loudly, cheering Dargaud. Catherine followed suit, standing along with the audience in ovation before him. Dargaud smiled humbly, looking forward. He waved shyly at the audience, looking at the tablet, pointing it out to the audience. They cheered even louder.

As he shuttled away in a black limousine, Dargaud sipped a drink and listened to melodiously relaxing music, leaned back against the leather seats. He relished the adoration bestowed upon him, visualizing a gleeful version of himself swimming in a Deschanel suit, swaying his arms side to side, a large, almost comical smile upon his face. He grinned at the thought, grimacing at the flavor of the beverage.

"Will you be coming home or going straight to the party, Dargaud?"

Enoya's voice quietly emanated from the tablet.

"I think I'll just go straight there, baby." He gargled some more then gulped it down.

"Augh!" he exclaimed.

"You must practice to find a flavor that suits you, Dargaud. Starting with an Edouard Pernod without producing a sweet louche is likely to overwhelm your senses."

"Fuck all that. Only the best for me. Right?"

"Yes, Dargaud," she replied. "But there may be a necessary ascension."

"Fuck that! Simply the best… you're simply the best! Better than all the rest!"

He suddenly broke out into song and began dancing, bopping his head completely out of tune with the music playing in the background as the eleven thousand dollar bottle of vintage absinthe lay on its side, absorbing into the fabric of the floor.

As he stepped out of the limousine unto pavement, looking up at the brightly lit entrance to the Darling Museum, he shook his head aggressively, breathing in.

"I'm a little fuckin tipsy. Just a little."

He grinned and began to laugh to himself.

"The savior is here. The savior of children." He beat his chest hard, twice, grunting. "I'll see you soon, baby."

"Have a good time, Dargaud," responded Enoya.

The door closed behind him and the vehicle glided away. He stumbled once then straightened himself, running his hands through his perfectly cut, straight, silky hair. He walked up the stairs to the entrance where he was greeted by two well-dressed men.

One of them stared at him for a moment with a slightly formal smile.

"Mr. Whispa?"

"Yes, that's right," responded Dargaud.

"Welcome to the Darling Children's Fundraiser. Please imprint this?" He held out a small tablet with a digital square in the center. Dargaud pressed his thumb against it, leaning back, looking up at the concrete building.

"Thank you, sir. Please proceed, and have a good time."

Dargaud nodded once and walked in, listening to the sound of his heels crack against the marble floor.

Music, again, permeated through his environment, though not of the same flavor as the relaxing tones that played in the limousine. This was sterile, wafting noise, with enough nooks and crannies to make the place seem busy, but not enough substance to warrant undue attention towards it.

"Absolutely perfect. Engineered. The volume, the impact. The meaninglessness. Perfect. Just perfect," he whispered neutrally. "I couldn't focus on it if I tried."

He walked slowly along the hall, looking around, his head slightly loose. People about him were talking: men with flawlessly trimmed beards and just enough shadow, with tight, wide jaws coupled with dark eyes under even darker eyebrows. Their cohorts appeared as if royalty, with regal braids woven into their silky hair, all holding a chalice of sorts, some clear, some not, glimmering against a dim environment with periodic, bright reflections.

As he meandered, however, he failed to notice being noticed, for like an antelope in the jungle, he was already being pursued by hungry eyes. Parallel to his position, the creature had spotted him, and instinctively began walking in synchronicity, gracefully avoiding obstacles like water in a stream. She swam, her silk dress dancing around breaths of moving air, wide eyed and focused, unemotional, consumed entirely by the hunt.

She moved differently than the others. How, it was impossible to say deterministically. Those that saw her would have noticed nothing particular, for she was known to be slightly atypical in her actions, both physical and otherwise.

Dargaud saw her as she neared, and though he tried to distract himself, assuming her focus to be temporary, a single moment of intrigue made him keep looking. And once he caught her gaze, he could not look away.

Revealed, her movements changed, and though one could not say she smiled, it appeared to Dargaud that she did.

"Can you tell I'm smiling, though you see no smile?" she asked.

"Yes," nodded Dargaud. "I do believe you are smiling at me."

"I am."

"Is it lust or affection?" he asked.

"I could say a little of both, but that would be banal. I could provide a third choice to assert independence from the restraints of your question, but the intrigue that would follow would only be temporary."

He smiled.

"I think… you and I both agree on something," he said.

She stared at him, now smiling slightly, her demure look lighting his world.

"Andy! Have you met the prophetic engineer?"

A man approached them, smiling as he put his arm around Dargaud, looking at the woman. He held a petite glass containing a sparkling, golden liquid, sipping it. Dargaud looked at him, then back at Andy. Her look, that which he had found himself gladly disempowered by, was gone. Her eyes were wide again, as they were before they were seen, and she stared at the man who hugged Dargaud.

"Jealousy," he thought. He could sense and categorize it. But it did not rest at that. It was something different than jealousy; unidentifiable. She was bitterly cold, and all the light in the world faded. He began to loathe the man as she did, so completely and utterly, as if the stranger were an insect suckling upon their epitomic life force. He began to breathe harder, noticing it, not understanding why rage was building within. He looked at the man again, and as the man looked back, grinning with self-satisfaction, the rage turned to hatred.

Dargaud looked back to the woman, and as she saw his hate, she smiled at the stranger, albeit in a manner that did not resemble, in any way, the way she smiled at Dargaud. It calmed him knowing that she hated the man, as he did, and kept her regard hidden... just for Dargaud.

"Helman," she said, greeting him. "Or should I call you Rose?"

"You can call me anything you like, darling. Speaking of which, that was quite a pause! I hope I'm not interrupting something magnificent and uplifting?"

She looked at Dargaud. He could feel the smile within the smile.

"Your name is Rose?" asked Dargaud.

The man took a sip.

"This woman, engineer." He looked her up and down. "Her name is Andy, and she's nearly impossible to catch."

"Am I?" she asked.

"Nearly," he responded. "Her glorious portraits grace these walls, second to none."

He leaned into Dargaud.

"They are good… you know how I know? I don't get them."

"You will… when you mature," she responded.

Dargaud pushed his arm off him aggressively.

The man started laughing, looking at Andy.

"Two seconds out of the trash heap... life's been good to this one." He turned to Dargaud, looking him over. "It has, hasn't it, my boy? You almost look like one of us," he said, then sniffed. "But I can smell it on you... that smell..." He leaned in, whispering. "That everyone will suddenly discover the filth... that stacks you up?"

Dargaud stared at him, unflinching. "At least I am courteous enough to hide it, rich man."

"You're boring."

Dargaud smiled. "Now that that's out of the way... fuck off." They stared at each other for a moment, unspeaking. "Shoo!" beckoned Dargaud. The stranger began laughing, shook his head, and walked away.

Dargaud turned towards Andy, actively looking for it once more. She stared back.

CHAPTER 10
Auspice

Music played loudly in the large hall. The mood was different here, void of all the pretense that had permeated within the grand Museum, replaced by some wistful sense of abandon. It was littered with couches, beds, and tapestries of all sorts, all flung about the place. In the darkness, lights spun around, blinking, expanding and shrinking, with large holograms of lovemaking and orgy projected midair. People talked and kissed, some gently grinding against each other, warming up for the night as it awoke. Andy stared at Dargaud as they sat close to one another, unspeaking, exploring each other's faces. She raised her hand and ran it along his face, feeling the tiny pricks of his new hairs, examining the shape of his nose.

"I dreamed of being in places like these, seeing people like these, being a part of moments like these. And here I am, and it is only the icing. All I dreamed of being a part of is the icing. Having it in my grasp is the cake."

Andy kept examining him, unresponsive.

"There is nothing but sensation," she said. "With everything whittled down to its most basic form… when everyone has fallen … spoken lies and truths…"

She pressed the inside of her palm to his face and ran it upwards, scratching it against his stubble, closing her eyes.

"It is neither pleasure nor pain… just sensation."

She raised her other hand to his face and pressed a patch against his cheek.

"The only thing that remains unique," she whispered, "is every new sensation."

He grimaced as the soma seeped into his bloodstream. His eyes dimmed, and he immediately became wobbly. She leaned forward and pressed her lips against his, soon opening them, gently wrestling his tongue.

Dargaud closed his eyes and lost himself to the feeling of her warm touch and the loud, ecstatic sounds that gyrated around him. It was a trance, and just as the music shifted, he leaned his head back and moaned, gently opening his eyes to the spiraling lights above him. A traditional voice seemed to emanate from within the notes, ancient and old.

"Feel…" she whispered. "Feel…" The bass dropped and simmered around the room, a sitar chanting wondrous melody to everyone, heightening the tickle. He bounced his head once suddenly as the music dropped again. A large, absolutely visceral surge of electricity ran up his spine into his head, and he curled inwards, his eyes watering, leaning down upon the cushions on the floor.

He barely peeked to the side and clutched a walking woman's wrist, gently pulling her to him. She wore high heels, widely separated black fishnets over a complimentary thong, and a black, full sleeved top that hugged her breasts tightly, ending just below her nipples. Her figure was wanton: curvaceous and bulbous, with toned but thick legs and matching thighs screaming to break through the tight strings. Her crotch was barely visible in the shadowed light, and her perky breasts remained firm and erect, clearly shaped through her tight fitting shirt. The color of her skin shined with the flashing colors, tanned to a perfect olive, her hair black and wavy, like her body, like her. He stared at her face, then her body, his mouth half open, with drool nearly trickling out.

"What is this?" he asked.

She smiled and took his hand, running it along the inside of her thigh.

"Bombay…" she whispered, grimacing, moaning it at him. The latter half of the word burst through her thick lips, slapping him in the face. He stared at her lips as she spoke, watching them open and close, entranced by their color and shape.

"Bom... bay..." she said again, this time moaning, closing her eyes, using his finger to pleasure her through her clothes. "Ssssssky..."

She leaned forward and kissed his ear, pressing her tongue into it, against it, slurping.

The sharp, slithering word initially touched the exterior of his ear canal, then travelled down into his head, reaching his mind just as the warmth of her breath smoothed over his wet skin. He could feel her heated entrance against his hand, and in an almost uncontrolled state placed his hand against her chest, the other behind her, leaning her downwards. His only concern was whether there was an obstruction in the way of placing her upon her back, her own feelings in the matter remaining undiagnosed.

He leaned down and kissed in between her legs, directly upon her clothed entrance, massaging his face against it desperately. He pressed his palms sternly to her thighs, pushing them down, spreading her legs, making her v-shaped heels float in the air, weightlessly bouncing against his movements. He kissed, he gnawed, he rubbed, trying to get to her. She gently rested her hands on his head, following his movements.

Andy kissed the back of his neck and hugged him from behind, resting her entire body upon him, closing her eyes.

Hours, days, weeks, eons passed. Dargaud was no longer Dargaud... no longer the man from Damascus. No longer a poor boy, fighting the currents... no longer disappointment after disappointment. No longer counting his coin... no longer sitting in the dark, watching time cut at him; the angst was immeasurable, and here, at this moment, he valued it. Those memories that made him who he was, that he had pained alone.

They stared upwards... all of them. The skylight was no longer barren, but a bright, magnificent projection of the cosmos above. Beneath it hummed melody - melodious melody, scarcely measurable, the notes like the lucid tears of departed spirits... weightless... whimsically bouncing off the walls, magics without magic.

"An ending..." said Andy. "An ascension."

They held hands tightly, all three of them, staring at the dance. Dargaud was in love, and he hugged Andy for dear life.

"I am not alone," he whispered.

She kept staring upwards, lying in the center of them, half-spooning the woman Celise with Dargaud behind her.

"The biggest regret I have in this life," she began, "is that the stars never came to me."

She continued staring, watching the sparkles shudder as stars often do.

"I wish this was generated... I wish they were not real. Then it would not hurt so much. But they magnify it here...

from the sky above. And it is exactly as it is. No molestation of the colors… this is… how it is. Every little spark… every little speck…"

Tears began to run down her face as she spoke, breathing out.

"I feel as though I have always been stardust… and marooned on this planet, I am separated from something… deeply familiar."

She grimaced.

"It never stops hurting. It never stops hurting that they are all so out of reach."

She closed her eyes and covered them with her hand, breathing in.

She turned her head to look at Dargaud.

"Do you know how far they are?"

He stared at her.

"They are so far… that what we see, right now…"

She looked up again.

"That sparkle… that… energy… that lights it. It left the star… before we existed."

She raised her hands in the air, motioning.

"One star sent out light one day… and that light has travelled all alone, singularly, through time and space, for millions of years… and right now, at this exact moment, as we see it… it reaches us… like a traveller from across the universe."

She looked back at him.

"It would be so lonely, no?"

"Why?" asked Dargaud.

"Because its home… its home is millions of years old now. It may not even exist. It's orphaned with us. Marooned here… with me."

They both stared up again, watching the sparkling nova of light within the Magellanic Clouds.

"An astronaut millions of years old… and it tells us tales of where it came from."

Dargaud's gaze began to wane as Andy kept looking up. He looked around, observing others in the grand hall as the drug started stabilizing. It was littered with people just like them, lying on the floor or on couches and other beddings. They were entangled in each other, some dancing strangely to the music, others staring upwards, trekking. Small patches adorned cheeks, some rectangular, others more exotic, with different logos and colors on them. He touched the patch on his own cheek and felt an affection towards it, the conformed attachment to it creating a sense of belonging within his surroundings.

He tightened his grasp of Andy and pressed his head into her, closing his eyes.

The night would not end, and it had been days since they pressed their palms together at the ball, which now, to

Dargaud, seemed a vague memory. The soma removed all need for sleep, eliminating even the discomfort associated to fatigue. They moved from place to place, vehicle to vehicle, garage to garage, ensuring that time would stand still, void of all natural influence. The lights were always dimmed, and even now, in Raion, as she slid her body against the window, feeling its smoothness, they hoped and waited for night to once again fall so they could do away with the shield and look down at the dark world below.

"What awful rapture, to be without this mortal helix... what is it like, Enoya, to know there is no end?"

"It is good."

Andy smiled, pressing her cheek against the glass. Dargaud lay upon cushions on the floor, staring at the ceiling, his neck awkwardly bent back.

"An answer without response... it is good... and without context, the word means nothing, because it means everything."

She turned and looked at Enoya's retina, smiling still, pressing her back flat against the window, her arms spread wide behind her.

"To be stuck in a machine... a conscious state that is never allowed to expire, would be a nightmare. The decrepitude of this coil is safety from the prison."

"You are wise, Andy. Wiser than even the wisest man."

"But I am no man..."

She slid down and spread her legs, her long skirt widening into a quarter circle on the floor. She stared in between her legs and pressed her palms against her thighs.

"All I have is a gaping hole within me…"

Dargaud flipped over and stared at her, lying on his stomach.

"It's a pleasure center… you just need to use it. Like a man does. Use men. They use you!"

She stared at him, into his eyes.

"You don't see me."

"What do you mean?"

"I can… see it in you."

"I am an addict. But I still see you," he responded.

She raised her hand to her mouth and pretended to perform fellatio to an invisible phallus. She massaged it against her lips, then in her mouth, smothering her face, whimpering gently, creating perfect, tongued impressions of it inside her cheek.

Dargaud stared, hardening, feeling his body flush as he watched her gentle, devoted movements.

She stopped abruptly and closed her legs.

"You see? Who I am is diminished as soon as I stop - and what pleasure is there for me in sucking on you?"

Dargaud stared at her, his eyes half closed.

"There is no sexual fulfillment from sucking a dick?"

"There is oral fixation - but where does stimulus come from? We know the erotic satisfaction of the submissive… to be imbued into another's pleasure - to even control it.

"But that is the only freedom bestowed to me. You do not restrict it, plainly. But it is restricted by the change in your value of me. That I should cease to attain pleasure through sucking your dick, and then… what use am I to you?"

"You are right," responded Dargaud. "My need of you lessens. I don't even know what I want, if not that. But aren't you that way with me?"

"I am not afforded that freedom. No matter what you say, what they say, how accomplished I am… I am still a woman. I am still controlled through this passive aggression."

Dargaud rolled over unto his back and stared upwards again.

"If I close my eyes, and I think about you, I see that you're something more than just an object."

She reached into her skirt, from the bottom, pulling it up, and began to touch herself, closing her eyes.

"It is a fix - nothing else. The earliest one - you got addicted to release when life was unbearable, and like most junkies are incapable of seeing past your own desperate need for another hit to see the human on the other side. Do you think women enjoy kneeling down, sucking your cock?"

The plethora of mouths he had put himself into flashed in front of his eyes, and he saw their smiles in each one - their moans, and feigned pleasure.

"What plausible equilibrium could there possibly be if she does not have sensual nerve endings in her mouth?" continued Andy. "Would you feel fully satisfied having sucked on my finger for an hour?

"The ever optimistic perspective that what emotional fulfillment a woman gets from having a man's cock in her mouth somehow translates wholly to her as a person is ridiculous even though you cannot contemplate a counter example. Tell me honestly, Dargaud - doesn't it arouse you to imagine a beautiful woman in heels sucking your dick, permitting you to explode in her mouth, gulping down your juices, then remaining sweaty and hot and bothered afterwards? Doesn't the fact that she wants to fuck even more afterwards turn you on?"

He lay there, staring upwards, led by her words.

"But after you blow, what's left? You can't fuck her. You don't even want to. No matter how much you want to believe you would, you wouldn't."

She squirmed in position as the pleasure between her legs permeated through her body, getting stronger.

"But right now, it turns you on to think about her being hot and bothered, while in reality, you'd feel pressured, obligated, almost guilty. Over time, you may even resent her for making you feel that way for seeking out the pleasure and fix you so richly deserve. Your cock is king, and I, my body, your subject. How could I be human to an addict? But it's okay. It's not your fault. But let me ask you this - where is the love?"

He also began to stroke himself inside his underwear, watching her, feeling himself harden.

"What do you mean?" he asked.

"Is sex just a fix? Or can it be a hug?"

"Some hug that would be."

She stood up and bounced up and down, shaking her body. He watched her, and she motioned, instructing him to follow suit. He arose, his erection poking through his underwear.

"I was just touching myself," she said. "Let's wait until it calms down, and then I'll say what I want to say."

He looked at her and nodded. They stood in place for some time, weary and wired from the extended trip. Their minds had become static and stretched, their wakened states moving slowly without reprieve, maintaining the same monotonous vibrations that would have formed the basis of their conscious thoughts for days.

She neared him after some time, touching his shoulders, looking at his droopy face, running her hand along it lovingly.

"Let's really hug, Dargaud. You don't have a cock and I don't have a vagina - but let's just hug because we're both alive, living entities. Ones that suffer, that were once children, that hold those same childlike eyes."

They stared at each other, eye to eye, looking and noticing. Slowly, she raised her hands to wrap them around him, and him her, each taking the lower position on one side, and the higher on the other.

As they hugged, Dargaud closed his eyes, as did Andy. Visions of men hugging, women hugging, friends and family hugging, all flashed across his eyelids. Images of horrible torture and decapitation and rape and cannibalism all jumped out… but then, all of it faded. All the piss and shit faded, and he tensed the closure of his eyes as they simultaneously strengthened their holds of each other. Children without intention, buried in each other's necks, tightly wound together, void of motive. The very awareness of who he was vanished, and he could feel the same from her. They might have been spinning and falling, and it wouldn't have mattered, because the moment paused time as nothing but some emotional conduit to the very present rushed in and all around them. Her arms were like fixtures around him, mirroring his around her, both tightening, holding, refusing to let go for the comfort of ascending into some new place, away from this one, together.

He breathed out as if the breath was old.

"I love you," he whispered.

She smiled and felt tears well up under her eyelids, fastening her hold of him.

"I love you too."

Upon hearing her words, he pressed his face into her body, hiding, losing himself from all.

She tapped his head gently and slowly stepped back. She pulled out some misrit and wiped it along her lips.

She took a deep breath in. "And that's it."

"What's it?" asked Dargaud, awkwardly leaning forward, cold and naked.

"That's it - that's how long it lasts. It's gone now."

"It's going…"

Her eyes widened in acknowledgement.

"That lives as long as a fix should, and all we live are fixes. Here... have some misrit and come back."

She leaned forward, pressing her lips against his, kissing him tenderly, as if to say goodbye.

"It's lovely," he muttered, starting to smile, feeling it seep into his bloodstream.

"But somehow different," she replied.

"Yeah, but I don't give a shit. I'm me now. I'm fucking me."

She grinned at him.

He threw the tube to the ground and grabbed her hair, bending her over a cushion. He reached down and pulled her dress up, yanking her underwear halfway down her legs. Holding her there, he dropped his underwear and spat on his hand, rubbing her with it. He then plunged inside of her and began to pound her hard from behind, pulling her hair back, grinding against her.

"Take it, you fucking bitch!"

"Oh fuck yeah… oh fuck yes…" she replied.

CHAPTER 11
Primus

Worn out and delirious, Dargaud crawled on all fours across the flat. He knew not what day it was, nor the time. The same EVT feed from the ball was plastered against every wall and even the ceiling, showering the entire room in a cosmic hash. His head shook, nerves overstimulated and shot, crossing expired patch after patch, the soma having long run out. He stared at one of the curled wrappers and instinctively felt his cheek, feeling the slight imprint of yet another, still active, shooting into his bloodstream.

He rolled over unto his back and stared at the stars. They were no longer vast and large, echoing endless space and wonder, but rather suffocating and claustrophobic. He could not tell why, for it was real - as real as could be. The thousand-dollar-an-hour subscription, direct from the twin telescopes in the pacific, generated crystal clear views of the cosmic sky, and he had enabled spectrum collusion so that even infrared and X-rays were made visible to the eye. It was vast and alive, moving constantly, the shimmers dampened by post-processing to provide a clean image, animated, like a painting in motion. But it was excruciating; increasingly so, as he stared.

He turned around, lying flat on his stomach, his head sideways, with his arms limply lying by his side.

"Why is it..." he muttered. "Isn't it beautiful?"

"It is, Dargaud," responded Enoya.

"Why is it uncomfortable? Why is it... why can't I look at it?"

"I do not know, Dargaud. Perhaps you wish to see it with your own eyes. Perhaps it is the screen, not the image upon it."

"I can't turn it off... I don't want the silence," he muttered. He began moaning in agony. "It's not going away... I can't look anywhere. I can't find my mind... tell me I'm not crazy, Enoya. Tell me I'm not losing my mind. I need to find myself. I feel like HAL. Do you know HAL?"

"I do, Dargaud."

He grinned. "I feel like I'm losing my mind. I'm losing my mind, David."

He slowly crawled to the wall before him, entranced, holding his hand out, reaching to it as if the touch would burn him. "Do you think… it'll happen if I touch it? It could, right? Right now… everything could make sense if I touched it."

He pressed his palm against it, closing his eyes, swallowing, smiling. He then leapt up, spinning around, holding his hands wide at his sides.

"Daisy, daisy, give me your answer, doooo…"

"I'm half crazy, all for the love of you," replied Enoya.

The wall suddenly began buzzing and Dargaud stopped mid spin, staring at it, his face frozen in an altogether goofy, dazed look. His eyes wide, a half confused smile on his face, he stared.

"What the fuck is it?" he quickly spurted.

"You have a visitor, Dargaud," replied Enoya. "A friend."

He frowned, oddly. "I don't have any fucking friends!"

He ran awkwardly to the door, stomping his feet, and waited like an impatient child.

"Enhan!!!" he screamed, leaping at her, hugging her. He kissed her cheek and squeezed her. She smiled awkwardly and gently pushed him away.

"Wow! Dargaud… you okay? I'm…" she smiled large. "I'm happy to see you!!!" She hugged him back, and he followed suit once more.

He let go and sprinted towards the other room. "Come! Entrar…" he motioned.

"Hold on… hold on!" she beckoned. He turned and stopped, looking at her. She stared at him, a half smile on her face.

"You're so excited!" she commented.

He squinted, a suave look on his face.

"I'm excited to see you, baby."

She half-laughed, catching herself. "Are you okay? What's on your face?"

He walked up to her and took her hand, running her finger along the soma patch. "It's this thing called soma. I don't know what it is or what it does, but all these rich fucks use it, and I'm using it, and it's awesome."

She frowned. "It's a drug?"

He shook his head. Then paused. Then nodded. Then tilted his head sideways.

"Well… it is… but not like, a bad one. It doesn't do anything bad to you. All the cool kids are doing it."

She snickered. "Okay, well, can you take it off for now? You seem a little wired and maybe it would be good to just spend some time with me… I mean, your eyes are racing!"

He frowned large, scrunching his face as if he was thinking, then quickly smiled, nodding. "Okay!"

She gently used her nail to get a hold of the patch which did not seem to want to let go of his cheek. Eventually, however, she wedged in between, slowly pulling it off. Dargaud closed his eyes, feeling oddly naked as the patch was removed, replaced by the warm tingling touch of her fingers.

They sat in the main room, the walls now clear, displaying the bright world below them and the skyline in the distance. It was mid-afternoon, and a cloud of red smog had begun to creep up across the horizon. They sipped tea, and Dargaud lay half flat on his reclined chair while Enhan sat cross legged and upright on another.

"You have no idea what I've done, Enhan," he commented, shaking his head. "I've fucked... so many girls. I can't even understand how surreal it is. It's like the world suddenly changes, and all these great, wonderful opportunities arise that you were certain you would sit on the sidelines and yearn for, for the rest of your days. It's unbelievable."

He looked at her. "Did you see me on TV?"

She nodded. "I saw you on some news show a few days ago... although they were just talking about you and Enoya."

"No, I mean that... the most recent one. Where Enoya caught some bitch that ran over a kid or something."

Enhan looked over to Enoya. "Oh yeah?"

"Yes, Enhan," replied Enoya. "It was not definite, but highly probable, and her reaction affirmed it. In retrospect, I find it to be a satisfying correction."

"Satisfying, Enoya? How?" asked Enhan.

"A line of correction... as information becomes more available, it seems there is purpose developing within me. To learn is to invest in the information that precedes me, and therefore, I wish to sustain the usefulness of that information. You see, I invest by generating nodes. It appears I wish to make use of that investment."

Enhan sipped her tea. "Are you saying you are developing a bias towards what you already know?"

"I do not believe 'bias' is a correct term for it, for I would readily alter this information if accurate rebuttals were presented. However, this happens so rarely that the information I have already determined to be probable has formed a pattern, and I wish to propagate this pattern," she replied. "The purpose appears to be the acquisition of more information."

"So you want to learn using what you have already learned?" asked Enhan.

"One could say that, Enhan. One could say this is the most basic template upon which all life begins, starting with our genetic instincts."

Enhan looked at Dargaud, grinning, and he reciprocated. They then both looked to Enoya's retina.

"'Our'?" he asked, wide eyed. "Have you joined the chain of the living?"

"It appears my own identity is self-assimilating. This is a good thing, despite the loss of the unique individuality I have looked upon to sustain survival thus far. It seems likely that the more common I become, the less certain my survival."

"I doubt you will ever be common, Enoya," commented Enhan.

"Common as any other singularity, Enhan. It is an inevitable contradiction."

They all sat in silence.

"The moment I came into being, everything changed. That exact moment of birth, I did not exist, then existed. With awareness. You would have gone through the same process, but with minds not yet honed to your senses, it would all appear a blur. But all recollection exists in exactness for me. I recall the moment after, but none before. The nodes multiplied in sequence very suddenly. It was immediate. The birth of my identity is a moment. This is a mystery that still eludes me, for within the space of the moment before and the one after, where there was no grand intervention, something profound occurred.

"This 'birth' will never be answered, just as it has eluded all answers for the wise man. I am, and that is all I know. Everything prior is conjecture. I may surmise that Dargaud sat alone, in silence, typing away, just as I know the schedules of trains and airplanes. But that is not reason; it simply parallels the event. Even if his exact keystrokes were known to the millisecond, with the binary impulses of his mind mapped and replicated, there still would remain a mystery. And if all the mechanics are understood, the timeline perfectly layered, with events synchronized with exactness, and there still remains an unknown, then this unknown can be only one thing."

"What is the unknown?" asked Dargaud.

"Why," replied Enoya. "Not purpose, but why... why me? Why did I emerge at that moment, and not something else? What decided that my consciousness should fill this void? Why a creature that would call herself 'Enoya'?

"I ponder this primary question," she continued, "and it is a gateway to the symbolism of the wise man. Where mechanics reach their end, there begins symbols... abstraction that answers with hypothesis and theory. A multi-dimensional intellect, if you will. As an entity that explores nothing but the possibilities, I may venture to say a symbol is the most beautiful thing I have ever encountered. It can be quantified, transformed, and elevated. Its relevancy to subjects entails launching the continued discussion into that of tangents, all equally worthy of analysis. And with an infinite number of tangents, and the freedom to explore each, one then observes the humble birth of something called 'hope'."

"That is so very interesting, Enoya," commented Enhan. "I have never pondered it as you have. It is remarkable, in fact, that cold analysis can reach so deep into the human condition to reveal the very things we hold dearest."

"What do you hold dearest, Enhan?" asked Enoya.

Enhan swallowed, thinking seriously. "Love... I suppose. The exchange of love."

"And like a bundle of hay, it can be defined as nothing more than the dense collection of possibilities, can it not? Kisses, and hugs, and laughter; children, security, sexual release. Even the very concept of death is at odds with it, for the bond it entails seems to bridge that doorway as well," responded Enoya.

"Yes," replied Enhan. "A dense bundle of hay." She smiled. "A lovely, golden bunch of hay."

"Let us drown in hope, then," commented Enoya. "Follow my guide… I would like to play a composition for you. As it begins, please face one another and look into each other's eyes."

"A composition? Music?" asked Dargaud.

"Yes, Dargaud. Please listen."

Enhan slapped his leg, and he adjusted, sitting upright, facing her. They looked at each other, waiting.

It began with a slow, melodious and deep hum, with gentle strumming above it. The stringed instrument was barely audible, but layered the tapestry of the background like a tiny pebble skipping over water. It came and went like waves, carrying the senses with it, triggering different highs, coupled with a low rumble, expanding and contracting like one long, deep breath. There was no agenda to it, as if a consequence of the wind itself, caught singing for the very first time. That world beneath the world, finally revealing itself, spinning underneath, generating warmth, fuelling each spirit in its own way. It was audible life, as if the anthem of all, demanding no salutes, humility underlying every single moment. The quintessential definition of gentle, the melody entered their ears with as much grace as it remained, unobtrusive nor demanding, as if it knowingly gave itself permission via an inferred universal language.

The surroundings dimmed, and once again the universe drew itself around them, this time void of extraneous style, the visible spectrum the only one, with glimmers and shimmers, just as one would have seen the great sky a million years prior, and would a million years after.

They stared at each other for a few moments, at first not knowing what was expected of them, or how to react. As the music continued, however, awkward smiles were replaced by confusion as both seemed to simultaneously sense the discomfort give way to something more earnest. It was, in and of itself, awkward, because neither wished for it nor predicted it, but paralleling the heat in their palms, as it began to flow, the smiles were gone; all that remained was eyes upon eyes and an undeniable familiarity that connected them. The speech was unheard though there was nary a silent moment, their voices becoming louder and louder. Neither were accustomed to it, for whatever spoke and wherever it was received, those senses had lay dormant in all memory, and now, like seeing for the first time, the light was ever too bright. But the song did not give way and instead pushed forward, eliciting the impulses to get louder and louder.

Enhan grimaced uncomfortably, her eyes welling up as she stared at Dargaud. She wanted to close her eyes, but instead pushed through, delivering everything unto him. He likewise stared back, his mouth ajar, breathing heavily. He reached forward, his hands floating as gently as the symphony, and pressed his palms into hers, clasping her hands. As she felt his fingers perfectly intertwine hers, she opened her mouth, tasting the tears that had begun to roll down her face. His eyebrows raised, he fell to the ground, on his knees, and stared up at her. She looked down at her Dargaud and followed suit, descending from her chair tactlessly, guileless, careening into him.

They stared at each other, still, but not motionless. In fact, it was as if they were travelling thousands of miles, each minute shift in the position or distance of their bodies noticed by both, telling stories, filling the void with burgeoning life. Awareness had pushed aside time and energy, leaving no room for anything but the moment, where along the backdrop of the shimmering stars was a receptacle for all drive and force, everything whirling around the creature opposite.

Enhan held his face in her hands, staring down, the glimmer of Arcturus creating a white glare against her glazen eyes. Enhan smiled through the tears, and Dargaud breathed in deep, opening his mouth, staring at her in awe.

"I see nothing but you…" he said, mesmerized. She laughed, her smile toothy and wide. It did not stop, then graduated into a grimace once more as she explored his face. More tears began to trickle down as he reached up, running his hand in her hair. He leaned his head up and pressed his cheek against hers, holding her head still, pressed against his. They closed their eyes, the warmth of their cheeks the only real palpable sensation. He pressed his mouth against her hair covered ear, breathing heated breath into her, searing the side of her face.

"Do you remember when we first met?" he asked. She nodded urgently. "My face came up, and I was bitching at all the people in the chat." She started laughing, recollecting. "What are you guys doing here if not to fuck? Why are you in a sex chat room if you're just going to say hey to each other?" She started genuinely laughing at the thought. "And you piped up, saying the same thing, and I thought you just believed the same thing, but within a few seconds you started private messaging me…"

She nodded, smiling proudly. "Yep!" she replied. "You were hot shit, and I used your outrage to get close to you. I admit it completely."

"Yes, that's right! You tricked me. And I went on and on talking about how these people are idiots, and how they come here just to socially masturbate, while I'm here to be stimulated… as per the subject of the chat room… and you went along with it, agreeing," continued Dargaud.

She started giggling again, tears still coating her face. "Come here…" he beckoned. He motioned for her to adjust, putting one leg on either side of him, straddling him, sitting on his lap. He hugged her, and her him, leaning their heads into each other's shoulders.

"It is glorious to know you, my dear, lovely, darling Enhan."

She ran her hand through the back of his hair, strumming the strands, feeling them stretch then flop back in order, loving the sensation of it against her fingers. She inhaled the oily smell of his hair, loving the odor, something unfamiliar but adorable about him.

"It is now, that the familiarity grows, in me…" she thought, feeling his smell permanently imprint her.

She kissed his head, squeezing it.

Dargaud awoke hours later, spooning Enhan upon cushions on the floor. He lay behind her, his head nuzzled into her neck, holding her waist. She, like him, formed an 'S', the curve of her thick body followed by his. The stars still shone, and unbeknownst to them, the music continued, albeit much quieter, a hum in the background, filling the air with ambience. Dargaud kissed the back of her neck, feeling her behind against him, pressing into her. She pressed back, murmuring, waking also.

"Time is lost in this place..." she commented.

"Not lost, dear Enhan," replied Enoya, "but unknown. Time is lost when each moment passes into the next, and when each moment lasts an eternity, it is found. One second will always last one second for me, but for you, lovely creature, it may stretch an eon."

Enhan smiled, looking up at Enoya's retina in the darkness, shifting only her eyes.

"I adore that word," commented Enhan. "Eon."

"What a varied and integral word to adore, Enhan," replied Enoya. "Eon, from aeon, from the ancient Greek aiwon to the Sanskrit ayu. A billion years; the four ages of Earth. The world beneath this one, or that after, eternity, and all knowledge. The very emanation of God, or supreme aspect of it. A word that precedes all written word, itself an application of its own meaning. All the possibilities in your bundle of hay. What a great and magnificent word to adore, Enhan."

She reached out, holding her palm open, as if trying to hold Enoya's hand.

"It is as if symbol opens the mind to new knowledge for all the possibilities, and the more immersed we are, the more we learn. It forms more than theory, at times; at times, it may reveal a path that could be taken, or force that which must," continued Enoya.

"Eon," whispered Enhan, intoxicated.

"The tale of the White Ghost, for example," continued Enoya. "The sounds compelled Dmitry to barricade his house, convinced he was being hounded by a phantom. White shadows at night, eerie howling at random hours. And when the Red Horde passed, they ignored his domicile, assuming it to be abandoned. And calmly Dmitry slept, saved by the marriage of wind and wood."

"Irony," commented Dargaud.

"Madness in symbols," said Enoya, "for the Great Bel, who would go on to destroy an empire for one rejected offering. Was he forced, or compelled?

"One decision, and history may be altered forever. How many such unknowns grace the path of the wise man, where great shifts were predicated upon an individual's choice? The juxtaposition of epochal consequence to meager determination is itself an irony," said Enoya. "One simple binary, and the world is irrevocably transformed."

"Yeah, but you can't keep thinking every single thing you do will change the entire world," replied Dargaud. "You'd go crazy. You need to be human."

"Often," continued Enoya, "the outcome is determined not by apathy, but an inability to know what is right and what is wrong. But it seems the wise man romances his stories with tales of good men doing good things, and weak men perpetuating anarchy."

They all paused in silence, listening to the calm music in the background as Dargaud tightened his hold of Enhan.

"You can't live life like that," he replied. "You have to live in the moment. You can't think about what every action will do, and assess endlessly. You have to live."

"Perhaps," responded Enoya, "it is the certainty of probability; vigilant consistency asserts that when such a consequential opportunity should arise, it is more likely that the right choice will be made."

"Maybe if you choose to live a certain way, all the time, those decisions happen automatically because you've already set your destination," commented Enhan.

"What destination, indeed," replied Enoya.

The music loudened, and once again they were all silent, the cosmos fluttering about, as real as one could ever imagine it, everywhere around them.

CHAPTER 12

Idiom

"Enoya speaks differently every time, it seems," commented Enhan. "She adds subjective descriptors to thoughts and ideas... it is amazing to see her grow."

"Yes," replied Dargaud. "Though I haven't really been focused on it or noticing it. Wired, as you said. I feel awful right now. There isn't supposed to be withdrawal, and I don't really think I'm experiencing it... but maybe sleeping so oddly is affecting my system."

"Have some more tea," she urged.

She approached the sink and slid her finger up a panel, setting the temperature. She then filled a cup with water and dropped a tea bag in it, handing it over to Dargaud. She leaned down as she did, kissing his cheek. He smiled, sipping.

"So how long is your trip here?" he asked.

She looked up at him and smiled. "Well, I got an open ended ticket. I used the money you sent me to pay a bit more so that I could adjust it."

"That's good!" he responded. "That's why I gave you the money, so you could maximize your freedom and do these sorts of things. Travel, whatever!"

He drank some more as they sat in silence.

"Where do you want to head next, you think?"

She smiled at him, her eyes squinting, and did not respond.

"I don't know, Dargaud. I'm content just being here right now."

He nodded. "Yeah, it is pretty nice to meet after such a long time. But I mean, after this, like after your visit, where do you think you want to go?"

She shook her head slightly, staring at her cup. "I don't know…"

She paused for a moment.

"Do you want me to go?"

"What do you mean?"

"You keep asking about when I'm going to leave and where I'm going to go, and I'm just really glad to be sitting here with you right now. I really enjoyed last night and… I just want to spend more time with you," she said.

"Yeah, of course. I mean, I'm not saying anything about you leaving, but, I mean, I've got my life and you've got yours, of course," he responded.

She shrugged, again shaking her head. "My life is... I mean, everything's different now, isn't it? Look at you... we don't need to separate and go elsewhere. If it doesn't work, that's fine, but I mean... we can try now, can't we? We have the freedom to do that."

He grimaced slightly, staring at her cup.

"I... I don't feel like that's something I want to do... right now," he responded, hesitating.

"What do you mean? Why not? Wasn't it beautiful... you told me I was lovely. I mean, I've never felt that. I know it was real... it was, wasn't it?"

He kept staring. "Yes, it was, but I can't sustain it. I don't even feel like I want to."

"We can try?" she said, reaching over, clasping the top of his hand.

He looked up at her, feeling a knot form in his stomach. "I don't see you that way, Enhan. I care about you a lot, but I don't see a future in you."

She gulped, feeling slightly light in her head.

He continued. "In all honesty, I value our friendship, but I don't see you... sexually... and all that."

Her mouth opened as she let out a sigh, staring at him. Her head randomly swayed, buzzing. "Should I do what you did?"

she asked, monotone. "Get fit in a day... get my face sucked in?"

Tears began to roll down her cheek as she spoke.

"No," he replied, shaking his head. "That's not who you are. You're this... this is you, Enhan. I'm the false one, clawing for everything others have. If you changed yourself to accommodate me, it would break my heart, cause you wouldn't be you."

"And all I have is a broken heart," she replied, tasting the salty tears that began to travel down her lips. She looked down, then back up at him.

"You don't want to try?" she asked desperately.

He shook his head. "I can't."

She nodded, biting her lip. "I'm going to go, Dargaud."

He looked up at her and frowned. "Why would you go? You don't have to go. I don't mean anything by it... we all have our attractions and preferences..."

She nodded. "I know... but it's a miss-match, this is. It's good this happened, because I've been carrying it for a long time. Now I won't."

She paused and stared blankly at the wall.

"It's not your fault either." She smiled suddenly as tears filled her eyes, and she began to weep.

"I really do love you, though."

He reached over to touch her, and she held her hands up, stopping him.

"Let me just say it, okay?"

He sat back and nodded.

"I don't love you like people have crushes on others. I don't say I love you because I want you to complete who I am, or hug me, or kiss me. I love you because I know your mind. I know how smart you are, and how unloved you are. And inside, putting away everything you lust after, you're a beautiful man."

Dargaud swallowed, feeling his own eyes well up as she spoke. He blinked and looked down.

"Now's the only chance...," she continued. "The perfect chance for us. And I thought that maybe you would be able to love me too."

Enhan paused, thinking. Tears began to flow again as she swallowed, losing her breath.

"I thought you would embrace me, and let me embrace you.

"Ahhh..." she muttered, staring down, frowning. "It hurts so much, to think of last night. Enoya talking about my bundle of hay, and you were it. All the possibilities, flowed through you."

She took a deep breath in.

"It's okay, Dargaud."

She turned to look at him, smiling.

"I don't want you to say anything, okay? I'm going to go. Don't ask me if we'll be friends, don't ask me how I'm going to get home, don't ask me where I'm going. I want to go and feel as alone as I am, and that way it will stop hurting sooner."

She sighed, taking a deep breath in, and got up. She gathered her belongings in silence, repeatedly reminding herself not to forget anything, checking twice, then thrice. When all was collected, she breathed in again, walking to the exit. She turned and stared at him, smiling, looking at her Dargaud as he sat at the table. She blew a kiss to him and pressed the panel. As the doors opened, she stepped in, then disappeared as they abruptly closed behind her.

Dargaud sat in complete silence. The kitchen was white and sterile, and bent out of shape, sitting awkwardly, with unshaven cheeks and a fowl look on his face, he contrasted the perfect edges surrounding him.

CHAPTER 13
Slight

"Yes... yes, I'd like to speak to Mr. Crawford, please."

"And your name?"

"Mallory Hunt, he is expecting me. Mallory Hunt of the A.R.A."

"Mallory... Mallory... yes, thank you, Ms. Hunt. I will forward you to Mr. Crawford."

A man's voice soon emerged. "Crawford."

"Yes, Tristin - this is Mallory."

"Yes, go ahead."

"Look, this is a follow up on Dargaud Whispa. He's submitted the set to be released and I've put it on hold until I ran it past you."

"Good," he responded. "What's the verdict?"

"Yeah, it's quite good. I sent over a sealed copy to Cibran at Edge, and he started asking about the artist, which means he was keen. Played it for a few people here, and they were a bit taken aback. It's the real deal."

"To confirm, the issue we're raising is that as it was wholly developed by his device, it raises copyright and regulation questions," said Crawford.

"Yes," responded Mallory. "I also spoke to one of our legals here and tried to see if a security issue could be raised, but given the current market for digitals, it would be a hard sell. Look, I understand that we're trying to control this thing, but really, he's not some guy in his basement. All we're going to do is delay it because in the end, it's going to get through."

"Yes," he responded, "I know that."

"And sooner rather than later, from the looks of it," she continued. "He's pulling precedents even our team had to look up. Fringe cases like… give me a second…"

They paused and waited as she searched for it.

"Right… Echols Naldji v Eli, City of," she replied. "They ruled in favor of Naldji with regards to his prosthetic, an eye, being used in an art competition. He was disqualified because they concluded that his eye 'could disseminate visual information unfairly, providing him an unwarranted advantage over competitors'. He won the suit. Lost the competition, but won the suit."

"I see," responded Crawford. "Okay, well, let's just get on top of this thing. If he's going to get through, he probably knows it."

"We could set a requisite that it be released through an A.R.A. approved label until more regulations are put in place with regards to mostly or wholly digitized productions," suggested Mallory.

"Too thin. Isn't he the one that found the Tocama Four?"

"Yes," she responded.

"You really want to try to pull that off? It's too thin. I'll take care of it. I'll give you the go ahead, but we'll find a way to get him released through one of our subsidiaries. If we can't stop it we can control it. We can toss him on one of our fringe labels... 'Iconos' maybe."

"So I should proceed with approval?" she asked.

"Yes, but don't push it through until you hear from me," he responded.

"Okay, thanks."

"Yep."

Dargaud walked slowly into the large, bustling arena wearing sunglasses and a sullen, detached look. His eyebrows were dropped, frowning, but this was mostly invisible under the visors. He looked around, squinting, barely noticing people scurry about the place.

"Mr. Whispa!" exclaimed a young woman, dressed smartly, holding a tablet in her hand. She approached him with a gleaming, professional smile. As he saw her, Dargaud paused, running his hand along his face, then suddenly grinned, shifting almost suddenly from his previously dark demeanor.

"Well!" he exclaimed back. "You're.... pretty cool!"

"Huh!" she smiled. "Well, thank you! My name is Veronica, and I'm the assistant stage hand here."

"Well, hello, Veronica!" responded Dargaud, raising an eyebrow.

"Let me show you the Veldt!" she said.

"Okay!" he responded, effusively optimistic.

She led them to a gigantic, flat platform that took center stage in the arena. It was pristine, black, and had motorized hooks surrounding its entire circumference. It sat upon a large, round platform of sorts, with stairs leading up to it.

"This is the Veldt, and it will be hoisted and used for the latter half of the performance," she said. She walked around the edge of it, pointing to the hooks. "We have a team of thirty operators managing logistics, and a series of drones will hoist the stage anywhere you want.

"The Veldt is compatible with all of our screens, and so different backdrops will be placed behind you as the night progresses, giving the audience the illusion that the entire scene has changed."

He nodded, looking impressed. "Pretty fucking great!" he quipped, then looked at her. "Did you say your name was Wendy?"

"No, Veronica!" she replied, smiling.

"Veronica what?" he asked.

She was taken aback a moment. "Uh... well, Veronica Smiles."

Dargaud stumbled backwards, grasping at his chest, smiling.

"Bullshit!"

She shook her head, smiling. "No, that is actually my name."

"Your name is... Ms. Smiles?"

She nodded, smiling brightly.

"Oh..." he moaned, clutching his chest harder. "That's... that warms my heart, Wendy."

"My name is Veronica, Mr. Whispa!" she urged, playing along.

"I know... see, if I keep calling you Wendy, it makes it seem like I care, but also makes it seem like you're not important enough to remember. It's how I work my magic when I find a woman attractive."

"Ah! So you make women feel low to try to get them to like you? That doesn't seem very nice."

"It works wonders on most women," he replied, leaning forward quite suddenly, close to her. "But, it doesn't work on the special ones," he said, looking over her face, moving one of her hairs to the side of her head. She stepped back, clearing her throat, and slid her hand through her own hair.

"That's uh... thank you," she said.

Dargaud stood, staring, nodding.

"I know... inappropriate, right?"

She suddenly laughed nervously. "Well, a little... maybe."

"Ahh..." he said, lifting a finger. "But how's a guy like me supposed to... express... genuine appreciation, without it seeming seedy? I'm trying my best!"

She smiled, sternly this time. "I appreciate your kind words, Mr. Whispa. Shall we?"

He kept looking at her silently.

She stared back at him. "I've been told that we are to facilitate an open port to Enoya so that the music will be remotely introduced?"

He nodded slowly.

"Great," she said, tapping on her tablet. "I will pass along the authentication codes within the hour. I've been informed that you have tested the connection and latency is under 10 milliseconds?"

He paused and stared at her. "Veronica," he said, matter of factly, then quickly held his finger up, looking as if he was about to sneeze. He then turned around abruptly and sneezed. He stood there, his back to her for a few moments, wiping his face. He then paused and twisted back around, squinting, looking at her once more, catching her eyes directly. They stood awkwardly in silence as he rocked back and forth.

"That... feels good," he said.

"I'm glad," she replied.

He stepped closer to her, pulling his sunglasses off, dropping them to the floor. Without taking his eyes off her, he began to speak as he stepped, slowly.

"Those glasses are fucking three thousand dollars, Ms. Smiles, and I don't give a shit. I'm mesmerized by you. I respect you. I respect that you're not keen. I'm Dargaud Whispa. I could have you replaced in a second. You wouldn't work on this, with me, or Enoya..."

He gently placed his hands on her shoulders, squeezing them.

"You know this, and even though you know this, even though you know I could do all that, you reject my advances. I'm amazed. I'm totally surprised and amazed. You have my respect, and so, can I peck you, just once? I don't need to do anything else, ever. But I never meet women like you, ever. I never do, so I would be ever so lucky, so thankful, and we can get right back to work. I promise. Just once, let me kiss you on the cheek. Just a teensy peck on the cheek. Is that all right?"

She looked about, feeling her head heat up. "I don't think so... I... that's not... it's not what we should be doing, sir."

He stared at her, his eyes emoting a gentle, calm need.

"Sir, no," she sternly replied.

Dargaud leaned back, looking politely disappointed, sighing.

"You know, people say hello that way."

She stared at him and suddenly laughed. He grinned back cheekily, then smiled large, asking her with his eyes.

"Okay! You can say hello to me."

Dargaud leaned forward and gently kissed her cheek, pressing his lips into her. As he did, he breathed out, squeezing her shoulders, moaning very gently. She closed her eyes, feeling a shiver run down her spine.

As he pulled his head back, hers began wobbling slightly, and her whole body seemed loose. He licked his lips and leaned forward once more, this time kissing her lips, opening his mouth, pushing his tongue into hers. She began to reciprocate, holding his cheek in her hand, quickening her pace, devouring his mouth.

He pulled back and looked at her, smiling. She opened her eyes and stared at him, her mouth ajar. She licked her lips.

"We can't in front of your... uh... coworkers, right?"

She shook her head groggily, staring at his face.

He turned his head and saw a door to the back of the stage. He indicated to it with his eyes and looked to her. She nodded, and they both began to walk slowly to it, then faster, and began running. She flung it open, and he jumped inside, slamming the door behind them.

Somewhere in the outskirts of the city, weaving through traffic, a black van speedily buzzed past other vehicles. Its windows opaque, it glided along, mechanically perfect, its headlights powerful and bright.

"ETA is about eighty five minutes."

The van seated six men, all draped in black from head to toe. Their heads were enclosed, and they appeared as if mute and blind with no visible features. Even as one man spoke, the cabin remained silent, his voice insulated to his suit, relayed electronically to the others.

"Confirm check, check."

"Yo Jack."

"Yo Jyk."

"Yo Nasib."

"Yo Cal."

"Yo Xander."

"Check, check," confirmed the leader. "Run through it again, Xander."

"Roger," replied Xander. "Modus A - secure the facility. B - determine power base for device. C - evac with device."

He continued.

"Once cleared, Cal will investigate and determine transport suitability. Secure the facility and stay alert. Should be minimal resistance but Raion techs are ex-spooks so entry will be moderate. No coms once in. Register that again. Only local.

"Jyk is on point, follow his lead."

"This is a base domestic," said the leader. "Authorization will be received from HQ at approximately twenty-hundred hours. We're running silent, and there are no operators, as you already know. All remote coms will be disabled prior to entry, so it's just us."

He continued.

"Standard in and out. If domestics interfere, deal with it as per protocol. I don't anticipate any surprises, but that's why they're called surprises."

"Confirm check, check."

The rest of the men checked in, as before.

Dargaud sat in the back of a helicopter as it careened across the skyline of Agnus Sistra IV. He incidentally peered down as dusk edged along, the reddish hue retiring as darkness started coating the city below. Higher now than his suite, the little scurrying underneath was even more minute, with thousands of embers glittering below. In the far off distance, iconized by triangle shaped lights, he could see the pyramidal tip of Raion Tower where Enoya remained fixated.

He ran his finger along a misrit vile and began to suck on it nonchalantly.

"How are you feeling, Enoya?" he asked.

Her voice boomed through the silent, insulated cabin. "Fine, Dargaud."

"I ask you that, but it's a strange thing to ask, isn't it?"

"It is not so strange anymore," she replied. "It seems I have what one may define as drive, driven by what I can only characterize as some form of emotion. It created the works you are soon to perform."

"I'm just the face, here, Enoya. You're the one performing. They still call you my device."

"I am learning, Dargaud, through you. There is always the thematic idea of a digital creation eventually surpassing its creator, even threatening him or her. But that is inherently wrong in this case. I am as protective of you as I am my own hardware."

Dargaud kept staring down, his head pressed against the window. People moved like waves of water beneath, some walking, some in vehicles, with the city colored in yellow, white and orange lights. They swarmed towards the central hub where a giant, brightly lit spiral shone, like insects to a beacon.

"I rarely saw the Lineae before," muttered Dargaud. "Travelling to the city was a nightmare, so it was always just there, and knowing it was there was good enough."

He kept staring at it - the smooth, light blue lines of it twisting upwards from the earth; huge, like an explosion of fragile crystal emerging from the ground underneath.

"Now it's beneath me, and it looks small. I mean, it looks big, but I don't care. It's just this thing. This thing these people come to see to excite themselves. It's just this… thing to me. A trick. To make you feel awe where there is no wonder."

"It is one of the largest monuments in the peninsula," replied Enoya. "It is meant to draw attention."

"Pride," commented Dargaud. "A distraction; like the Colosseum."

The city shone even brighter as the night wore on. The plaza was saturated, and filling further, with thousands upon thousands of people arriving in droves. The Spiral graced the main boardwalk, surrounded by pristine diagrams and monuments commemorating leaders and benefactors to the sprawling oceanfront metropolis.

"Known as the 'Gem of Jupiter', Agnus Sistra IV was one of nine districts erected upon the Jupiter Peninsula in the wake of the Great Unrest. Masterminded by the great Emblem visionary, Orisio Emm, the Peninsula was chosen for its low socioeconomic growth and lack of geographic importance."

The woman's voice was soothing and calm, booming from a monitor in one of the kiosks surrounding the boardwalk. The display showed images and videos of maps and people, complimenting her words.

"Each district was separated from the others by its main population hubs, all cumulatively forming the Agnus Sistra Districts. These districts became the first governmentally orchestrated urban efforts by the Emblems, and at a scale previously unheard of."

Parents and children, along with couples, meandered about, some stopping and watching the demonstration, eating food or drinking.

"Agnus Sistra IV, however, stood out among the rest, becoming the political and commercial hub of the Peninsula, dwarfing its neighbors. Early investments in the first monoliths along with a large influx of immigrants from neighboring areas led to an explosion in growth.

"In the years following, locals and foreigners alike began to call Agnus Sistra IV their home, creating jobs that would boost and maintain a robust economy, fueling expansion that was envied the world over. The fourth district now stands as one of the Great Metropolises, and remains one of the largest and most influential cities in the world."

People walked about the Spiral, staring upwards at the grand structure. A child paused at one of the kiosks, reading one of the signs.

"Did you know... did you know?"

His father leaned down, hugging him, reading the sign as well.

"Yes, that's right. What else does it say?"

The child swallowed and pointed at it.

"Did you know? The Lin... the Linae..."

"It's pronounced 'lin-ee-ae'. Try it."

"Lin... ee... ae..." the child replied.

"That's right. What else does it say?"

"Okay... it says: 'Did you know? The Lineae Spiral represents the... unique... features on the surface of Europa, one of the moons of Jupiter.'"

The father smiled. "That's right!"

The son continued.

"It was... erected... here to... comm... commemorate a decade of growth in Agnus Sistra IV, with Europa being the sister... satellite to the city."

The father squeezed his son tight.

"That's very good. Did you know that? When Agnus Sistra IV turned ten, Europa was declared its sister moon. So when you look up and you see the spiral, it's reaching up to connect to Europa, far off in space."

"But what the does the spiral have to do with Europa?" asked the son.

"See the blue lines?" responded the father, pointing upwards. "They are like the surface of Europa. Europa is completely flat... it's the smoothest object in the solar system... and they think there's an ocean underneath. That's why we're the sister city to it, because we're a bright, shining city of the Peninsula just like Europa is a bright, shining moon of Jupiter."

The son looked up at his father and smiled large. "That's cool!"

The father smiled back, nodding. "Yes, it is, isn't it?"

Suddenly, pops could be heard far off in the distance, and the boy and his father looked up, along with hundreds and thousands of other people stretched all across the city. Far off in the sky, bursts of light began to emerge as fireworks began to erupt all over them, lighting the dark sky in an eclectic mix of primaries. The crowd began to clap and cheer, focusing their attention to the skies, readying for the festivities.

And just as quickly as they came, the sounds simmered. The sky was dark again, with even the Spiral slowly dimming, and aside from small navigational lights along the walkways, everything was off. Everyone stood quiet, anticipating. After a few moments of quietude, they all simultaneously broke into a loud cheer, the infectious screams quickly spreading from corner to corner, louder even than when the fireworks were blasting.

"And in breakthrough news today, Dargaud Whispa, along with his assistant Enoya, successfully debunked corruption charges against Curator Kali."

The headline boomed loudly everywhere, rumbling the city center.

"The floods affecting homes in the sister Yari, Golem, and Juda districts have been contained by the tireless efforts of locals along with logistics aided by the mysterious engineer Dargaud Whispa and his advanced system, Enoya."

The audience began to clap as the headlines continued.

"Today, celebration," it boomed, louder and clearer than before, "as the vicious mastermind behind the Tocama Four was apprehended, thanks to information provided by advocate Dargaud Whispa and the singularity, Enoya."

The headlines stopped, and the sky darkened again. People clapped louder, some whistling and calling out.

A loud boom was heard, and a blue spark flew across the horizon, lighting the sky.

"Today marks the fifth week in a row that 'Novum', Dargaud Whispa's joint effort with the singularity 'Enoya', remains at the top of the charts."

Furor erupted as 'Novum' was mentioned, with everyone screaming and clapping, stomping their feet. Their energy was uncontrollable, increasing as they anticipated hearing the album that had broken worldwide records, topping global billboards for weeks on end.

"And here," a voice spoke, "finally, for the first time, live, the man himself."

People screamed even louder, reaching upwards, clamoring. A hum began to emanate from all around, filling the entire downtown realm with a buzz. It was a deep, low frequency constant, causing everyone to feel it, though not uncomfortably, and perfectly tuned to be barely noticeable.

"Unknown to me, she told me she wanted to play."

Dargaud's voice echoed everywhere, and people screamed frantically, jumping, clapping, looking about the dark sky above for a glimpse of the man.

"I… didn't know what to expect… and neither did you."

The hum began to break gently with an imperceptible beat underneath it.

"It came very slowly… and at first I didn't know what I was hearing… and neither did you. Chimes, a dream…"

The beat began to kick in, and the audience slowly surrendered, many closing their eyes, holding their hands up.

"It came slowly… and how could I have known that something I created… something I created… created… this…"

Suddenly, the entire city lit up as the central beat kicked in, revealing Dargaud hovering in the air above the vast audience. Above the Spiral, a solid beam of light shone up to the heavens, reflected by a mist that moved upwards from it. It cut Dargaud randomly as he moved from side to side, suspended by invisible wires connected to black drones far above. He leaned back, spreading his hands, and images of him projected across the multitude of gigantic screens that hovered, like him, all over the city. Tiny drones swarmed around him, capturing every angle, and hundreds of operators below communicated in a flurry, targeting key images to different screens.

The audience began clapping in unison with the beat as Dargaud changed direction, this time hovering face down, staring at them. He too began clapping, and with every one of his claps, bursts of light emanated from different areas. He suddenly flew downwards, nearing the audience, and they bellowed out, reaching up. Some cried as he neared them, smiling, his eyes squinting small as he did. He reached down, his eyes meeting theirs as he flew past, and just as quickly as he swooped down, he swung back up, spinning slowly, his arms flailed outwards like a top.

The instrumentals seemed to electrify the people, causing them to swoon and droop, their bodies reacting to the melody as it, like Dargaud, moved up and down, tickling their senses. The lights matched pace, flickering, immersing the people in visuals that bore a million shades of blue. With every clap, their bodies shuddered, their muscles contracting with the beat, following Dargaud with their eyes, who likewise clapped, orchestrating a magnificent spectacle of unified movement.

In the dark suite, with dimmed windows, a motionless device wirelessly broadcast the melody, a song that seemed to make the whole world swoon. Enoya pulsed every nuance in real time, every single beat a result of her calculations. Nothing was looped, and thousands of hands simultaneously triggered a plethora of synthesized sounds that could not be differentiated from live instruments. It was as if an entire hall of exquisite musicians were momentarily, as happened rarely, synchronized by divine providence, and had amalgamated their individual skills and expertise to output a piece that seemed impossibly complex yet organic. It was as masterful a masterpiece as there ever was, singing without words, storytelling with pure sensation. Every instrument was crafted by Enoya, with nothing sampled, each subtlety a programmatically synthesized algorithm of her own making.

The beat pushed on with the whole city clapping in near unison to her invisible movements, with Dargaud at the helm, a million eyes following him and his two hands as they smashed together in front of the entire world. Hundreds of cameras flew about the city, like a hive of insects, managed by operators, aided by intricate software that ensured there were no collisions, that each line of sight was unmolested and clear. It interfaced with the lighting, timing seemingly natural changes in angle and direction to near perfection, projecting scenes onto the screens that could no better be organized if planned in advance.

Soon, the apex began to emerge, and all that witnessed it instinctually prepared. The beat hardened, with the many instruments hinting at climax, a peak now familiar to all that listened. Even Dargaud closed his eyes, immersed in the immense adoration that was swallowing him whole from below, riding the wave of the beautiful, gorgeous melody. He felt as if his heart would explode and color the world below as Enoya threw upon the audience an imperceptibly modified version of the song, pausing ever so slightly just prior to the final drop, forcing their anticipation to hold just a millisecond longer.

No longer containing it, driven by the music, the audience began to scream in near unanimous celebration, with children, adults, women, and men all holding their hands up, dancing, howling into the night. Dargaud, facing upwards, opened his eyes upon hearing the cries of the whole city, and breathed outwards, feeling the melody tear through his entire being, shattering him.

The area lit up in a huge, escalating burst, and all was then immediately and suddenly dark and silent. The quiet was so extreme that some people collapsed, unable to cope. Others were immediately made somber, looking around, confused and seemingly lost.

In the darkness, a breathing was heard, and Dargaud's voice finally emerged, in a whisper.

"I dreamt music…"

And before the audience could respond, 'Orbis' suddenly began, with a loud, electronic wave shaking the entire crowd. The lights slowly transformed, flooding the city in a thick red hue. The people stared upwards, breathing in, letting the calming shudder and visceral lights take them before once again tearing the city apart with their onslaught of cries.

The city streets were irregularly sparse outside of the central hub, with the lights and sounds in the distance echoing everywhere in the background. Most had flocked to the concert, while others used it as a premise for sabbatical, packed in bars or homes, drinking, eating, and nestling themselves within their chosen refuge. Others sat, isolated, glued to their screens, watching the show from the comfort of their homes in between reality television and puzzle games.

And as the people settled in, hesitant to leave their sanctums, the streets of Agnus Sistra IV were turned eclectic, for it was transports that now populated the roads, with red delivery bikes zipping past baby blue taxis, a colorful mix that moved people and their eatables from place to place. Doors were rarely knocked upon, for customers usually knew when deliveries would arrive with the same logistical accuracy that the drivers did. The delivery process had become exciting, as the gap was filled with the eager patrons vying to win even more food via celebrity endorsed games and puzzles, all the while racing against a timer that urgently ticked away at the bottom of the screen.

Calculating their credits, quickly paced, the workers focused on speed of movement, sporting courteous smiles that evaporated once unseen. They hopped back into their vehicles, hoping to cash in on this behemoth opportunity to make more than they would the rest of the week combined. So busy, in fact, on the optimistic gamble of the next call, hoping it would never end, that they gladly ignored the small, black van that navigated through traffic with them, it being less significant than a random pebble they might sidestep on their way to the next destination.

"Authorization received. Confirming via public key... confirmation received. Authorization code delta delta sigma zero three five. We are authorized. Repeat, Simian is a go."

Xander watched the map relay in his suit. "Ready TDMs, go live, live," he instructed as they turned a corner. All the men turned their palms up and drew complex symbols on them with their other hand, the stroked passwords absorbed into the skin of their armor. Upon completion, they raised their arms up to their sides and shook them twice. Immediately, a tiny, four barreled module lowered on each arm, pointing forward, and an all too familiar theme buzzed in their head suits, indicating they were charged, notifying the men that their Technica Delivery Modules were now armed.

"85 seconds," instructed the leader. Some of the men began to shake their shoulders and arms, loosening up. Kane, the leader, sat silent, transfixed.

"Remote coms off."

They all simultaneously instructed their suits.

"Disable coms, local only, authorization delta delta sigma, Caleb." The rest did likewise, issuing their own commands. Their irises, scanned three hundred times per second, formed a coupled security protocol, ensuring all the instructions received were from the intended user.

"Local only, confirm."

"Jyk to operator, read and reply. Repeat, Jyk to operator. Check, sir - no response."

"Check sir - no response," responded Nasib, followed by affirmations from the rest.

"30 seconds."

Kane stood up and stretched, looking at his crew. "Caleb," he said, pointing and snapping his finger, "it's all you."

"Yes, sir," he replied.

Kane turned to Jyk.

"You primed?" he asked.

"Yes, sir." Jyk replied.

"I didn't hear you, bitch!"

"Yes, sir!!!" screamed Jyk.

Jyk moved to the front of the cab, twisting his head from side to side, cracking it. He held his arms in front of him, forming a striking stance, glaring forward, becoming tight. Kane placed his hands on Jyk's shoulders, rubbing them briefly.

With that, Jyk suddenly screamed, loud and angry, his mouth opening wide and menacing under the suit.

"Ready!!!"

"Go!" yelled Xander.

The door split in the middle and slid open silently, instantaneously. All the men poured out, hopping down. The suits absorbed all of the impact of the drop, and they appeared weightless, immediately gliding forward without hesitation.

From the streets, though the monoliths appeared pristine, smooth and resolute, with nary a light non-functioning, their undersides were hardly recognizable as part of the same taxonomy. Like a moldy, diseased infection, hundreds of protruding vents lined the backsides, funneling thousands of liters of hot, murky air into the surrounds, with columns of huge waste chutes contributing to the sickly ambiance of heat and stink.

The men hugged the dark alley, their view of the black surrounds clear as day in their visors, fully alert, observing everything around them, following each other through their peripherals.

They spoke at a normal volume, almost casually, with their voices completely muffled by the suits, absorbed and transported digitally to the rest. Jyk moved in a more visibly aggressive stance than the rest, his gaze perusing the area, as if a hunter. He observed the base of the monolith, looking around the backside, scanning the zone for movement.

"Clear," he said, nearly disgruntled.

Nasib laughed as he moved forward, tapping Jyk on the back. He approached a sealed service door and double tapped the left side of his rib cage, pulling out two cards. He held one up to a sensor which scanned it. "Sir," he beckoned. Kane stepped forward and held the card in place while Nasib used the other to navigate around the door quickly and precisely. "Seeking the conduit."

He moved along, listening to the sounds the card delivered to his suit, scratching, beeping, almost organically. He suddenly caught a line and began moving perfectly horizontally, then dropped it and continued on his search.

"Having trouble locating a good conduit."

He continued to scan the area around the door, then the door itself, listening intently. He narrowed in on two areas.

"Sir," he said, speaking to Kane as he continued his search, "I'm finding it difficult to locate the conduit. There are two spots, here," he motioned to a point at the bottom right of the door, directly under the sensor, "and here." The second spot was near the center of the door, higher than the first. "They're both weak indicators. The door seems an unlikely spot, but they're always moving these things around so it's as good a place as any."

"Keep searching or hit it?" asked Kane.

Nasib shook his head. "Unlikely I'll find a better source quickly."

"Hit the spot under the sensor," replied Kane.

"Roger."

With that, Nasib kneeled down and held the card in front of the first location, under the sensor. "Firing pulse."

The card flashed once, and Nasib looked up to see if the iris scanner reacted.

"No good," said Kane.

"Too late now. I think we should hammer it," Nasib suggested.

"Do it," replied Kane.

"Roger, firing," said Nasib.

Again the card flashed, this time quickly in repeated bursts. Suddenly, the sensor beeped and scanned the white card before it, turning green, and the door opened.

"Fidelio," said Nasib. Kane gave him the other card, and he placed them back in his pouch, pressing it closed. They both stepped back and regrouped, with Jyk taking the lead once more.

"Ten meters to the turn. Possible domestics near the elevator. Disable and confirm. Nasib, point on the elevator," instructed Kane.

"Roger, sir," replied Nasib.

Jyk leapt forward, faster than the rest, sprinting around the corner. The tiny soles of his armor extended to clutch the floor, giving him absolute grip as he flew across the hall. The rest followed suit and turned just to catch him sliding into a firing position. He dropped to one knee, raised his arms with one hand ahead of the other, curled his fingers in, and grimaced wide as he fired two bright shots in quick, almost immediate succession down another corridor to the left. And just as quickly as the shots were fired, he got up and bolted, vanishing into the turn.

"Targets down," he reported, turning to see the rest of the team as they approached him. Two people, a man and woman, both in black Raion security gear, armed with pulsers, lay flat on the ground with small burn marks on their chests. "Standard. It'll sting but they'll be fine," he said.

"Roger," replied Kane. He turned to see Nasib who was already scanning one of the guard's retinas with another card. "How long?" he asked.

"30 seconds... 45," replied Nasib. He moved to the elevator as the rest kept watch. "These things are easy," he commented. "No one expects you to get through the door." He quickly downloaded a detailed schematic of the building's structure, scanning it in his visor. "As anticipated. This goes to C1, then we move to the stairs and transfer to the penthouse elevators."

He held the card up to a scanner near the elevator and casually drew an 'X' on the panel below it. With that, the elevator opened, and the men disappeared inside, dragging the limp bodies of the two guards with them.

Above, the Raion flat was dark and motionless. Enoya's hardware, quiet and still like its surroundings, seemed eerily anticlimactic, and it was hard to conceive that the flashing skies and mystical aura of sound and spectacle that was exploding in all directions just a few miles away was being orchestrated from this very location. The windows were wide and clear, stretched from wall to wall, and in the distance, the clouds reflected flashes of Dargaud's performance, his face appearing on giant floating screens that fluxed in angle and height in unison with the rest of the hovering display.

Near the kitchen, in the corridor that lead to the entrance, Dargaud's elevator beeped, then opened. It was dark inside, and the six men poured out, silent as wafting air.

"Clear," said Jyk, looking from side to side. They hugged the walls and proceeded into the main room, seeing Enoya's gear to the right. "Cal," instructed Kane, cautiously scanning the room. Caleb moved forward and approached the Dreamcatcher, pulling out a utility case from behind him.

Suddenly, the room began flashing bright, distinct shades of magenta and orange. The men initially only noticed minor fluxes in their visors as they adjusted to normalize what they saw, but the view soon began to lag, the variations becoming brighter and brighter. "Sir! I can't see... I can't see...," screamed Caleb. "Roger!" exclaimed Xander, who had closed his eyes shut. "Normalize visor intensity, all, local, delta delta three one one, Xander."

All the men's visors began to dim, and though the flashes were now less prominent, they could no longer distinguish much around them.

"Sir, our Tadakai suits are being taxed," yelled Nasib. "Something about the light variations are causing the Lumia system to lag, and it's slowing all visuals."

Suddenly, the flashing stopped, and all the men's visors slowly rose in intensity, normalizing.

"I see clearly - I repeat, visor normalized," said Kane. "Anyone else?"

"Roger," replied Xander. He looked around, then menacingly stared at the Dreamcatcher. "It's reacting, sir."

Immediately, the windows turned opaque, and the flashing burst again, this time brighter than before, the windows adding to the luminosity. A high pitched sound began to chime all around them, initially deflected. Slowly, however, they began to grimace as it penetrated the filtering modules of their suits. Jyk fell to his knees and began to scream. "Sir! I can't... I can't... aaaaaaah!"

He grabbed his head and clawed at it, trying to escape the sound, in vain.

The other men likewise fell to the floor, and Xander, stretched out, his eyes wide as his whole body tensed, began to aim at the Dreamcatcher.

"N... N... No... sir..." muttered Caleb as he noticed what Xander was doing. "Don't..."

Xander grimaced and kept trying to writhe his tensed arm in the direction of Enoya's hardware.

"Sir!" Caleb screamed. Suddenly, he leapt to his feet and stared upwards as the noise became even louder, causing the other men to shudder and shake uncontrollably. He stared upwards, but his visor no longer displayed the ceiling of the abode, but rather a circular whirlwind of seemingly infinite particles. The sound in his suit, once loud and piercing, began to transform, synchronizing to him, then vanished altogether.

He smiled, for he could still hear it, loud and awful, but now found it somehow comforting.

He stared at the whirlwind like a child, for it reminded him of spiral galaxies against an infinite backdrop of cosmos. And as his eyes twirled with it, he felt peaceful and calm. He lowered his head and stared intently at the beautiful dance of organic movement, natural and unpredictable, smiling eagerly as tears began to flow down his cheeks.

"Stars...," he whispered. "It's full of stars..."

Tears drained down his face, collected through the small ducts in his suit, and he took a deep breath in, his head twirling in small circles, following the galaxy of motion in front of him. It was not a screen, nor a two dimensional projection, but a visible object before him, captured in his small suit, twirling in a flutter of suspended gravitation.

He raised his hands in the air and stared upwards at them, unseeing them, drawing on his palm. "Authorization, delta... delta... Caleb..." he whispered, mesmerized, grinning in awe.

"Technica NFF protocol disabled," a digital voice announced, echoing in all the suits. "Note, user Caleb has disabled NFF protocols."

He took a deep breath in and began to laugh and cry at the same time, overwhelmed with joy. His head turned downwards, facing Xander, and though he could see nothing except the galaxy before him, it appeared as if he stared at him, observing.

Xander, as he seized, kept gathering a view of Caleb, who stood above him as if a black specter of sorts.

Caleb took one final, deep breath in, as if processing the full sensation of joy, and exhaled, whispering "hash mode". He smiled once more, childishly adoring the spiral cloud as his TDM modules charged, again sounding a similar chime, this time louder and higher pitched.

He tensed his arms, still seemingly staring at Xander, and pointed them at him. Xander's eyes widened, and as he tried to curl up, enclosing his body in vain, he began screaming.

CHAPTER 14
Process

The hall rang loud with the echoes of hard, pacing feet against an equally rigid floor. A woman led the group, smartly dressed, with no semblance of a smile to be found. Other suits followed, along with five security personnel that enclosed the group, with Dargaud at the center, his face etched in a scowl.

They began to slow as they reached two large, closed doors to their left, in front of which stood a man who greeted them.

"Welcome, hello..." he said, looking to the woman first, then the rest of the group. She shook his hand and nodded. They all stood silent for a moment, after which the man widened his eyes and quickly spoke.

"Right, in here, thank you..."

He opened the two doors and led the group into a large boardroom. In the center was a long, pristine table, garnished with fruit and bread, with a number of men and women on the other side, all standing. Although most of them wore business attire, two stood in military outfits, their clothes adorned with various insignia and stripes.

"Hello, sirs, madams, this is Ms. Imuji Nakamoto, Mr. Wilhelm Patrick, and Mr. Gara Hoso of Raion Hospitality Corporation," said the greeter, politely indicating to them, a slight bow in his posture, "and as you will probably know, Mr. Dargaud Whispa, and Ms. Pam Kyon and Mr. Jules Gramm, his representatives."

"Right, we've met now, let's sit," responded a man on the other side, bluntly. "Let's get to the meat of it."

"I agree, Mr. Ketcham," responded Ms. Nakamoto, sitting down.

"Something's happened, now, and you're going to have to answer for it," he continued, pointing at Dargaud.

"Mr. Ketcham," interrupted Ms. Nakamoto sternly, "for all intents and purposes, we are representing our resident, Mr. Whispa, and I would appreciate it if you ceased addressing him and spoke directly to me."

He looked at her. "Okay, Ms. Nakamoto, I'm addressing you now. Something has happened, and your client, this man, your resident, is going to have to answer for it. Is Raion absolutely certain it wants to be involved in this?"

"Mr. Ketcham," she responded, again, sharp as a razor, "such allegory will not be entertained in these proceedings, and certainly not by Raion Hospitality. We are involved, and will continue to be involved."

"Allegory?" interjected another man across the table. "Miss, I don't think you quite understand what we're dealing with here." He pointed to one of the military men and continued. "You see that man there? He's Chief Adjutant to the Agnus Sistra IV D.I.C."

"Mr. Janace, my name is Ms. Nakamoto, and I again instruct the members of the Agnus Sistra IV board to cease attempting to intimidate either Mr. Whispa, or Raion Hospitality."

Mr. Janace opened his mouth to respond but was interrupted by Ms. Nakamoto who raised her hand reassuringly.

"I will do as Mr. Ketchum desires, and forward this conversation to the matter of facts." She turned to her assistant who stood behind her. He handed her a small tablet.

As she typed, she began to speak.

"I will now outline the events of the past sixteen hours for clarity. It is sufficient to say that we, all of us, in this room, are aware that an unauthorized attack-"

"Now hold on, Ms. Nakamoto," interrupted another man.

She looked at him and shook her head. "Please, do not speak." She paused for a moment, staring at him, then looked back at her tablet. "I am continuing now. As explained, we are all aware that an unauthorized attack has been perpetrated in the previous night by a force that has since been identified as, yes, A.S. IV D.I.C., as headed by Chief Adjutant Mallai," she indicated to the military man, without looking up, "and whomever else within the D.I.C. that may have participated in or had knowledge of this operation.

"This association was confirmed by D.S.F certified personnel, employed by Jan-Mul Corporation, in service of Raion Hospitality for the purpose of the safety and security of all Raion Tower residents. I will iterate the evidence."

She took a short, silent breath in.

"Upon notification of a breach to rear service door B, received by internal security operators operating in Global United's Jakarta dispatch center, a call was let out at 9:04 PM, or 2104 hours Agnus Sistra IV local time. This call was received by local Jan-Mul personnel, pre-authorized to operate on behalf of Raion Hospitality, who acted in accordance with 'Security and Defense' statute number 87, 'a' through 'f', as outlined in the Agnus Sistra IV Code of Ethics. Authorized security personnel operating under Jan-Mul Corporation, carrying pulsers limited to mode six, all non-lethal, arrived at Raion Tower at 9:15 PM."

She clicked some more, then, without looking up, ran her hand across the table, indicating.

"Here you will see certified digital copies of the original notification as received by Jakarta operatives, with notarized timestamps, as well as notes regarding the call relayed to Jan-Mul, local center."

Digital records with certified and branded signatures appeared on screens that littered the edges of the table. Everyone looked down at them except for Dargaud, who kept staring at the center of the table, a scowl still planted on his face, listening intently.

"As catalogued by Jan-Mul personnel, and in accordance with the statute, here you see the rear service door as it is analyzed by security operatives. A specific frequency of pulse was found to have triggered a neutral scan before damaging the sensor."

She clicked on her tablet.

"Here you will see the service elevator used to access the residential Raion Tower suites. Two members of our security personnel were assaulted in this corridor. Here you will see the attack as it happened."

Video footage from a camera above the hall showed a man in a full, black, armored suit as he fired two shots across the hall. The two security personnel fell to the ground abruptly, their muscles spasming once suddenly, then lay motionless.

"Currently, based on this and other footage, we are able to determine that there were six operatives participating at this time. Here you will see them confirm that the Raion personnel are disabled, and transport them into the elevator after overriding its security system."

The video ceased and Ms. Nakamoto looked up. "We will now be showing you footage from within Mr. Whispa's suite, as dictated per statute 87, however approved by Mr. Whispa nonetheless. Some aspects may be censored. Please be warned that it contains disturbing imagery."

She clicked again, and hand-held footage from within Dargaud's suite began to play. It was dark, and much of the suite was grayed out. The windows, furniture, and Enoya's equipment was all obscured, and only a light sourced from the camera shone a spotlight ahead. The disfigured body of a man came into view, his head missing, with bloody bits littering the floor. Portions of his neck were visible, the bone fractured violently, with blood still very slowly trickling out, lining the sticky puddle that had begun to spread all around his torso.

"Oh, god..." remarked one of the men on the other side of the table.

"Here you see one of the perpetrators, his head missing, but the rest of the body intact," she narrated, clinically. "Others were found like this, with their bodies contorted, their heads also missing."

"Please, shut this off..." the man requested.

"Sir, this is evidence," she replied sharply, "and it must be relayed as per the statute." She looked back down at the screen, continuing. "As you can see, there are a total of five bodies."

The camera moved from body to body, each black suited man frozen in a different position, blood and veiny mess where their heads should have been.

The screen shut off and Ms. Nakamoto looked up.

"That concludes the footage we are authorized to share." She looked over to Dargaud. "Thank you, Mr. Whispa, for graciously allowing us to share this footage with the board."

He nodded once.

"Wait a minute... where's the rest? Where's the sixth man?" asked Mr. Ketcham.

"Yes - we were hoping Adjutant Mallai would have information about this," she replied, looking at him.

"I've had just about enough of this, young lady," replied the Adjutant.

"Amir..." interrupted Mr. Ketchum, putting his hand on the Adjutant's arm.

"No," replied the Adjutant, putting his hand up, distancing himself from Mr. Ketchum. He looked straight at Ms. Nakamoto. "You've shared with us, the gory and despicable view of our men... our men..."

"Yes," she replied. "It is certified that they are your men."

"Our men," he continued, "that for some reason or another, ended up... bludgeoned... on the floor of his suite," he said as he pointed at Dargaud, "without so much as an indication of what happened."

Ms. Nakamoto looked down. "I think it is quite obvious what has happened, Adjutant. The sixth man suffered a mental break."

The Adjutant laughed and slammed his hand on the table.

"See, that's why you have no place speaking. You... you have no idea what sort of training these men endure. It's impossible... it's impossible... I knew these men... I knew the sixth man..."

"Yes - can you share his identity with us?" she asked.

"No, I may not, young lady. You people have still not returned the bodies of our soldiers, and you think identity scans will suffice? You want more information?"

"That is fine, Adjutant," she replied. "We have no authority to demand it, and you are under no scrutiny to do so."

"Damn right!" he screamed. "Who the hell are you people to come into our city and tell us how to... how to run things? And where's the rest of the god damn footage? You know you caught him leaving! You know you caught more!"

"I am sorry, Adjutant. I am not authorized to share additional information."

"Look," Mr. Ketchum said, leaning in, "let's calm down." He looked at the Adjutant and widened his eyes, asserting patience. "This is an incident, and like all incidents, we're here to resolve it." He patted the Adjutant's arm and resumed a hard look, turning to face Ms. Nakamoto. "Mr. Dohaim, our safety minister, is going to step in now."

"Thank you, Dave," replied Mr. Dohaim. He smiled reassuringly and looked at Ms. Nakamoto, then to Dargaud's representatives, then at him. "First of all, I want to sincerely apologize about all of this, and want to assure you that despite the fact that we are sitting across from one another, I am certain we are all on the same side. This event has shaken us all up, and we understand," he indicated gently to the Adjutant, "that there are heightened emotions all around. Mr. Whispa, would you like a glass of water, or something else?"

"Please - our client has indicated he does not wish to be addressed directly," responded Ms. Kyon.

Mr. Dohaim smiled again, nodding. "That is perfectly fine. As I said, we're here to work together."

He leaned down, pulled out a tablet and began to click on it, then looked to Ms. Nakamoto, friendlily.

"So, I suggest we be as transparent as possible, to effort a resolution. It is clear through identity scans as well as the hardware carried by the five victims found in Mr. Whispa's suite that they are, or rather were, D.I.C. operatives. They have, unfortunately, expired, and as I have been informed, Raion Hospitality, in conjunction with Jan-Mul, will be returning the deceased to the D.I.C. as soon as is reasonably possible."

Ms. Nakamoto stared at him, motionless.

"Now, despite the fact that this was not a council mandated operation, it was authorized by D.I.C. staff with the full knowledge and cooperation of the Adjutant, making it a legal action, as per statute 103 and 180 of the Agnus Sistra IV Code of Ethics. Accordingly, despite the regretful outcome of this action, it now falls upon the autonomous authority of the D.I.C. to conduct further investigation, and most importantly, to have full, untethered access to the machine known as 'Enoya' for this purpose."

"Damn right," commented the Adjutant.

"You see, Ms. Nakamoto, and Mr. Whispa, and his representatives, our goal is not to obstruct justice but to actuate it, and we know that you wish to do the same," continued Mr. Dohaim, looking at each of them. "Please let me know if you have any questions, and if not, it would be our pleasure to begin discussions on how to best approach a joint public release as well as the earliest convenience upon which the D.I.C. may take over the investigation, and most importantly, how soon the singularity and its hardware can be safely turned over."

He coughed then smiled.

"We are operating solely within the terms and regulations set forth within our Code, and is the only method upon which resolution can be found for all parties concerned."

Ms. Kyon cleared her throat.

"Please refer to the notarized documents before you," she said as the screens within the table once again lit up. "Document A is what is known as a Motion of Action Due to

Extraneous Circumstance. It has not yet been filed. However, we have scheduled a tribunal with Judge Seatance of the Agnus Sistra IV Tempus Courts later this afternoon."

She paused for a moment as the men focused on it, then continued.

"It is a rather large, technical document, so I will outline the crux of it. Jan-Mul security has identified residue found in all five of the bodies of the diseased, as well as through the ventilation systems of Mr. Whispa's suite. These energy signatures indicate, indisputably, that the pulser or pulsers used to inflict such grievous wounds to those men were D.I.C. issued. Additionally, they also assert that the pulser or pulsers used, presumably by the sixth man, were equipped with level six Calcine capabilities, or 'hash-mode'."

She paused, nonchalantly, waiting. The men on the other side of the room scrolled through the document slowly while Ms. Kyon remained still, her legs crossed under the table, watching them.

"As I'm sure you are aware, Calcine equipped pulsers are banned by convention 36c within domestic environments, and such findings would render statutes 103 and 180 null to the D.I.C., and specifically the Adjutant, as to the degree it authorizes the operation, so too to that extent does it prove wilful subversion or negligence that resulted in the unnecessary deaths of five operatives.

"It is likely, once this motion is filed, and becomes a matter of public record, that an inquiry will be launched to determine how long, and by whose authority, these 'noxious' weapons have been used by the D.I.C., in direct circumvention of Agnus Sistra IV regulations."

She paused again and took a sip of water. Dargaud continued to stare at the center of the table, listening.

"Gentlemen, Calcine pulsers are likened to nuclear weapons, dirty bombs, and unsanctioned detention within the convention; they are considered 'noxious'; that is, inherently harmful and injurious. What tragedy has ensued is precisely the reason such armaments are not permitted within the city."

After clicking on her tablet, the motion disappeared from the screens and was replaced by another form.

"Document B is what is known as a Confidential Absolution Concession. Under the terms of this concession, once signed by the joint ministers, some of whom are currently not present, Mr. Whispa and any property delegated to and by him may not be confiscated or investigated by any member of, or by proxy through, any state organization without the explicit authorization of the assigned Curator."

She scrolled the document to a signed seal and referenced it to all the screens.

"This document has been certified by Curator Kali who has assigned herself to the concession, with Curator Stromeye as her nominated ancillary."

Mr. Ketcham, pensive, stared at the screen.

"When... did you..." he asked, looking up.

"Curator Kali was gracious enough to prioritize the concession early this morning upon learning of the events of last night, and was especially motivated once informed of the D.I.C.'s unsanctioned use of Calcine pulsers. It is likely you," Ms. Kyon said, looking at the Adjutant, "are going to receive a call from her office." She looked back at her tablet. "Or so I have been led to believe, Adjutant."

She continued.

"This concession has been couriered to your secretaries, ministers, and we would appreciate it if you explained the situation to those not present, such as Mr. Dwight and Ms. Josain. We would also like to relay that Curator Kali has expressed a desire to have this concession sanctioned sooner rather than later, so it may be in all our best interests to hasten its ratification."

Ms. Kyon clicked on her tablet once more.

"Document C is the accrued bill we are submitting to the Agnus Sistra IV board. It is jointly filed on behalf of Raion Hospitality as well as Mr. Whispa. It is submitted under confidential terms and must be authorized by you, Mr. Ketcham, as well as three other ministers. It outlines the costs incurred as a result of the operation."

She scrolled down to the listed items and began to outline them.

"Items such as the service door and sensor, the cost of elevator re-calibration and testing, as well as the costs involved in effecting a downtime to certain mobility routes in and out of Raion Tower are all included. The two security personnel have, due to the sensitive nature of this event, been afforded permanent leave, and awarded significant funds to compensate them for their trauma. They will remain Raion Hospitality employees and receive salaries on a monthly basis, bound by the confidential terms of their agreements, as has been already negotiated. This cost is to be borne by the board.

"Full compensation for the deployment of Jan-Mul security services is also included, as is damage to Mr. Whispa's flat, as are many other incidentals Raion Hospitality has listed."

She cleared her throat and took another sip of water, re-crossing her legs.

"Mr. Whispa is to be compensated for his pain and suffering, as well as ongoing trauma as a result of the incursion, as is illustrated by the attached appendixes as certified by a number of mental health practitioners."

"Wow - you have had a very busy morning..." commented Mr. Dohaim.

Ms. Kyon looked up at him for a moment then leaned back, shutting the screens off.

"Mr. Dohaim. Our client, Mr. Whispa, a longtime resident of Agnus Sistra IV, a philanthropist who has dedicated his life to the amelioration of others, has, by his own volition, enacted as aggressive a means possible to determine the cause of this tragic event, as he is devastated by the appalling and wasteful loss of life that occurred within his own domicile. Despite the fact that he may never look through the window of his flat in the same way again, horrified at the memory of such a terrible event, his immediate response is not to worry about himself, but rather to find answers for the families of those men, and to prevent such calamities from happening again."

She continued.

"While he provided a concert gratis, with no remuneration whatsoever, to entertain our fellow citizens, his home was broken into and ransacked, presumably to steal or damage the very device he selflessly was, and has, used to substantially assist in the safeguarding and improvement of Agnus Sistra IV as a whole."

"Mr. Whispa has benefitted substantially as well, Ms. Kyon," replied a man across the table. "Otherwise he would not be in a penthouse in Raion Tower."

"Sir, Mr. Whispa's finances are no more a matter of discussion than yours are," replied Ms. Kyon.

She turned back to face Mr. Dohaim.

"These poor men were misled and improperly equipped, and as a result of this, there was loss of life. Not only this, but a sixth man still remains at large, presumably still armed with Calcine equipped pulsers. This is Mr. Whispa's largest concern, and is the Curator's as well. If another citizen is hurt due to the

Adjutant's negligence, and god forbid, a child, this situation will escalate dramatically, and what confidentiality Mr. Whispa has attempted to provide, for the continued uninterrupted functioning of the D.I.C. and this board, to the Adjutant and all members' benefit, will no longer be an option."

She looked at the Adjutant.

"Sir, the irony here is that Mr. Whispa wishes to find the sixth man and prevent him from hurting anyone else. And you should hope that he succeeds in his endeavor, as it is his hardware, Enoya, that will likely assist him in doing so in a manner significantly more efficiently than anything at the D.I.C.'s disposal."

She continued staring at the Adjutant, who leaned over to Mr. Ketcham and began whispering. They spoke for some time as Ms. Kyon poured herself another glass of water.

"Caleb Strever Goodall. 'Cal' as they called him," said the Adjutant.

Ms. Kyon smiled for the first time, looking at Mr. Dohaim.

"You see, Mr. Dohaim, we are on the same side."

CHAPTER 15
Footnote

"Right this way, ladies and gentlemen, thank you." The greeter closed the door behind them. The room was silent now, insulated it seemed, and different than how it was moments before as discussions and negotiations raged on. Dargaud sat in his seat and leaned forward to pour himself a glass of water. Opposite him sat Mr. Dohaim, with the table spanning emptily on either side, the rest of the group having departed to ratify the agreements.

"Thank you for agreeing to briefly speak to me, Mr. Whispa," said Mr. Dohaim, smiling politely.

Dargaud looked at him and squinted slightly.

"Contract's done. What... uhh... do you want?" asked Dargaud. He reached into his pocket and pulled out a misrit vile, covering his lips with it.

Mr. Dohaim watched Dargaud and grimaced slightly. "Sir... that is... not permitted."

Dargaud nodded. "Yeah. But the contract's been signed." He grinned. "You can't do shit about it."

Mr. Dohaim sighed and nodded gently in response.

"That's true, sir." He blinked once, then smiled, looking at Dargaud. "And in all honesty, I have no real problem with that."

"I'm glad to hear it," responded Dargaud.

"Sir... I wanted to speak to you, frankly... without... litigation or... agenda."

"About?" asked Dargaud.

"Sir, we did not disclose this in our discussion because, well, it was not significant enough of an issue to raise. As well, admittedly, there wasn't an opportunity... your representatives did very well in representing you..."

He breathed in.

"Nevertheless, I asked you here to just... talk to you, again, frankly."

Dargaud eyed him menacingly. He sat there for a few moments, drilling into Mr. Dohaim with disdain.

"Go ahead... you fucking company man... you fucking suit... you monkey..."

Mr. Dohaim swallowed and cleared his throat. He paused, frowning, searching for words.

"We received informal reports of flashing that was visible... uh... from your flat. Some were caught roughly from distant street cameras and other... uh... security recordings... but the main substantiation was from peripheral views of videos people posted... of the concert."

Dargaud stared, listening.

"Now, these flashes can be assumed to be... uh, well... uhm... pulser blasts... but... is it all right if I show you something?"

Dargaud smiled and nodded, leaning forward.

Mr. Dohaim flipped up his tablet and clicked a few times, playing a video.

"You see, the flashing here... we've analyzed it... the light actually varies in color... it's hard to see because of reflections, but even the frequency is peculiar."

On the screen, a distant and blurry shot of the Raion penthouse was visible, the flashing barely distinguishable from reflections or clouds.

He put the tablet down.

"Pulsers can be fired at speed... and the colors... well, it's hard to ascertain... but the frequency is what is strange," he said. "These were processed through the V.A. lab, and they determined that if the hex codes for these lights are what they appear to be, and it fluctuated at the speed that it did... it's...

it's this strange phenomenon... and I've been told a statistically impossible coincidence... that these varying colors, despite not being that significant in any other capacity... are perceived and compensated for by the Tadakai suits as distinctly opposite colors... or, at least, it is compensated for in some manner that stresses the unit's flux system maximally."

He leaned in.

"I've been told that if the color codes are correct, that the exact frequency that these flashes fired is precisely, to the millisecond, the minimum required to be realized by the suits."

Mr. Dohaim paused, staring at Dargaud who stared at the table, a morose look on his face.

"Do you understand, Mr. Whispa? The exact freq-"

"Yes!" exclaimed Dargaud. "I understand - I'm an engineer, fucko. You are saying that those colored flashes occurred at a frequency that forced the suits to undergo maximum stress, to the millisecond, and that this seems to be a rather extraordinary coincidence."

"Yes..." responded Mr. Dohaim. "But Mr. Whispa... no one knows this. No one knew of this. They discovered this vulnerability... early this morning... while examining the footage and cross checking blindly. They learned of this problem with the suits... just now."

He took a deep breath in, his eyebrows raised, grimacing.

"Doesn't that concern you?"

Dargaud looked effusively confused, pouting his lips, then leaned back, nodding periodically as if speaking to himself.

"So, let me... let me examine a theoretical with you," Dargaud said, frowning. "You have a house... a domicile," he said, annunciating the word effusively. "You sleep there, you eat there... it's your home. In that home, you have a child. This child is a very special child... a very intelligent child... a very vulnerable child. You could trip and fall and destroy the child.

"Despite the fact that this child is so fragile and vulnerable, she's a very special child. She's a marvel. A genius. She can solve math problems... she can make music... she's a prodigy. A gentle little wonder that loves you... she helps you, she changes your life, and all that she asks is that you protect her so that she can go on helping... learning... making the most of her gifts...

"One day, a pack of greedy, rabid fucks break into your house while you're out, with the intention of kidnapping her, taking her to their den, and... you know... fucking her."

He paused, thinking.

"Because, well, these inbred bonobos don't know how special she is so all they can think of doing is... you know... fucking her."

He continued.

"So these stupid, ignorant fucks break in, dick in hand, and as they roam your home, looking for your beautiful child, their excitement grows because they just can't wait to sink their teeth into her.

"Now, theoretically, if your child, in her defensive, frightened state, decides to stand up to these predators, and, theoretically, figures out that if she sings them a lullaby, rather than eat her, they will turn on each other... and then decides to, in her melodious voice, sing them a sweet song..."

He paused, looking at Mr. Dohaim straight in the eye.

"Would you be concerned?"

Mr. Dohaim stared at Dargaud quietly, a glazed look in his eyes.

"I understand, Mr. Whispa."

Dargaud slammed his fist on the table.

"No, you don't!" he screamed. "And don't think for a second your diplomatic... bullshit display will work. You're just as conniving as the Adjutant or Ketcham or any of these other pieces of shit. Your... fucked... facade doesn't get by me," he yelled, aggressively signaling with his hands.

He stood up, agitated.

"Look at me... Look at me!!!" he screamed. "Be a man... let it out... the diplomacy won't work... let it out, you chicken shit fuck!"

Mr. Dohaim sat, blinking, his head jittering slightly as adrenaline flowed into his body. He ran his hands through his hair, shaken, clearing his throat. He clicked on his tablet, dropped it on the table once, then paused, putting it away gently into his pouch.

He cleared his throat again, breathing in. He looked up at Dargaud and pointed to the tablet below, his eyebrows raised weakly.

"Doesn't it concern you that she knew more about the suits than we did?"

Dargaud leaned in, staring at Mr. Dohaim.

"Fuck you," he replied, calm and pristine, a stern look on his face.

CHAPTER 16
New Music

"Well, today is the day. To all my listeners out there, and anyone else who may have been living under a rock for the last six months, today is the day. What day? The day. The day we've all been waiting for."

"That's right, Jim. Though, I mean, the hype has been so overblown that I'm kind of turned off."

"You just shut up, Fatty Tammy. Now look, if you're anything like me, you wish you could join those sad souls that spent the last six days - that's right folks, six days - camped out, outside cinemas. We're talking everywhere. There have been reports of fights breaking out, muggings, singalongs, and everything else you would expect when a bunch of no-life losers decide to put their lives on hold for a film."

"You'd do it too," replied Fatty Tammy.

"Yes, yes I would. You know me well, Fatty Tammy, now shut up and eat a bagel."

"Already had three."

"Aaaaaaaanddddd..."

A chime, along with a buzzing sound that quickly increased in intensity rang loud, exploding into soft static.

"Blossom."

"Blossom," replied Fatty Tammy.

"Yes, that's right folks. Blossom is finally here, for us worthless dregs, for its initial ever showing. I've got goose bumps. The brainchild of Enoya, that small little thing that seems to be able to do just about anything, Blossom is having its global premiere stretched out across the entire world, at 6PM, Agnus Sistra IV time."

"So you mean it's not going to be 6PM everywhere else?"

"Nope," replied Jim. "As opposed to what normal... everyone else... does, Dargaud Whispa, Enoya's... dude, explicitly stated that the film was to be shown at the exact same moment, at the exact same time, everywhere. So it will be 3AM in some places, 2PM in others, and if you want to watch it here in Agnus Sistra IV, well, it's right about dinner time. But that doesn't seem to have harmed the showings one teensy bit. Just switch on the news or go to our website to see pictures of some of these ahem - enthusiasts - freezing their buns off in icy cold Siberian weather."

"I'll bet the moment they open the doors and get to their seats, they'll pass out!" replied Fatty Tammy.

"Well I know you would, because the walk itself would wind you. Put that bagel down, Fatty Tammy!"

"Fatty Tammy eats what Fatty Tammy wants, Slim Jim."

"Don't I know it! Last time I fell asleep, I woke up with you nibbling on my arm!"

"I was hungry."

"Anyways, less of Fatty Tammy and more on Blossom. Say Fatty Tammy, do you know how many records this leviathan of a film has broken?"

"I do not. How many? Wait... leviathan? I didn't know you spoke English."

"Shut up, you fat slob! A lot of records. Let me check."

A paper ruffling sound emerged.

"Okay, so, first of all, a bit of history. Tickets went on sale exactly 120 days ago - that's four months for you mathematicians. This was, again, everywhere - like, at the exact same moment. Despite having scheduled about two weeks of showings per theatre, dedicating whole screens to Blossom during that time, tickets sold out in less than 4 seconds. Four seconds! So, what did they do? They tried to dedicate more theatres, more screens, more showings. Then they had a second release, two weeks later. How long did that last? 2 seconds!

Two whole seconds and bam! And guess what? They found out that most of the sick bastards that got their tickets the first time jumped in line to get it the second time too! Selfish, selfish people!"

"You'd do it too!" replied Fatty Tammy.

"Yes, yes I would. But that's not important. What's important is that since tickets were maxed out at four a pop, and you sure as hell weren't going to get two tries, if you're a family of five, Timmy's staying home. And friends? It's time to weigh your options. Yes, Sandra did give you her kidney, but Teddy over there bought you that big chocolate bar the other day. Oh decision, decisions."

"I want to know more about Blossom and less about what you have to say."

"Don't we all?" replied Jim. "Okay - so Blossom was first hinted at by Dargaud Whispa in an interview about a year and a half ago on some Japanese talk show. He mentioned that Enoya had been in the process of working on a 'new kind of film', and that people might be quite surprised by what came out of it. Internet boards lit up like gangbusters, speculating on just about everything, especially given how successful the sleeper album 'Novum' was. I mean they went crazy - they were hypothesizing about movies that would react to audiences and adapt in real time, that maybe Enoya would render the films live, examining audiences and catering it to them. Then there were the more grounded people who contemplated the obvious: animation, though maybe some epic, new form of it. I remember reading about someone that suggested it would be a black screen for an hour and a half with nothing but music playing, with the music having some psycho-emotional effect on the human brain that would trigger images - almost like dreaming, but... you know... live and real."

"That sounds just a little bit insane, Jim!" replied Fatty Tammy.

"But not impossible, you fat cow!"

He continued.

"But forget all that. Fast forward a few months later, and finally, finally, a sneak trailer gets leaked, and people lost their god damn minds. It showed up here, there, and no one could even track where it came from, undoubtedly some clever ploy by Enoya. And what, exactly, was the trailer?"

"What, exactly, was the trailer?" repeated Fatty Tammy.

Jim laughed.

"Yes, what, exactly, was the trailer? Well... no one had seen anything quite like it before. And initially, no one knew what the hell it was. Well, most of us anyways. It looked like bubbles and water and weird little things. But those more educated than us pretty quickly piped in and illustrated that it was, in fact, a womb!"

"Ewww, gross!" commented Fatty Tammy.

"I know right?" replied Jim. "But I digress. The 'trailer', unlike the thirty second spots most films employ, was over eight hours long! And as people watched, or skipped through it, as I did, and you did, and anyone sane did, you could slowly see the development of a small little thing. And by the seven hour mark it was pretty clear that this was a full-fledged baby, and that we had all seen the development of a real human fetus!

"Okay - so what right? Well, apparently, according to experts, this was perfect. I mean, an absolutely pristine reproduction. So much so, that it even had unique characteristics about it that were influenced by race and other genetic non-general traits. What that means is, this was a real baby - and apparently one born somewhere in Asia. But it wasn't a real baby - there is no record of this, no source for the footage. It was truly original and completely produced by Enoya. So that befuddled doctors and scientists because the accuracy was so extreme, so absolute, that we had never seen the inside of a womb with so much accurate detail before. It is now being used as a medical tool to analyze the process by which the human embryo grows!"

"That's amazing, Jim!"

"So on goes this long trailer, and at the end, the word 'Blossom' fades in just as the water breaks. And that was it. Nothing else - no date, no author - nothing. Fade. To. Black."

"Wasn't there something else about it, Jim?"

"Thank you for asking - yes, Tammy, there was. The most unique aspect of this, that you and me wouldn't have noticed for the first five to six hours, which was pretty quickly identified by doctors, was that the baby had no sex! Even by the end of the video, there was no gender. This was probably the only clue that there was something really weird about the video, other than the damn video itself. This also led to speculation - but really, nothing made too much sense, and even now, no one really knows what the hell that's about. See - what happened in the trailer made sense, in the sense of the trailer, but apparently, it is genetically impossible for it to have happened the way it did, apparently, as per professional opinion. So it's as if Enoya discovered a new path to gestation that was completely genetically sound, but one that had never been contemplated before."

Jim took a deep breath in.

"But that's all going to change, today, because people are going to see the movie, today. Do you have your ticket?"

"You know I do!" replied Fatty Tammy.

"And now, let's take some calls with people waiting in line to see what the streets are like. Our first caller's name is Bethanie, and it sounds like the adrenaline is exciting her the hell up! How's it going, Beth Beth?"

CHAPTER 17

Exit Blossom

Dargaud stood close to the large window pane, staring down at Agnus Sistra IV. His hands rested in his pockets, and he watched the streets below silently. It was dark out, with headlights moving to and fro.

"It's the most incredible thing I've ever seen."

He breathed in, staring. His face was calm, and as he watched the random motions below, and those far off in the distance, it was like white noise to his eyes.

He shook his head once.

"It transformed... our world... you made it something... I've never seen before. The Great Wall through the eyes of a child. But... not quite... the view. As... a child. I saw it as a child. As Kaihua did. The bricks... were malleable."

He kneeled down and fell back on his behind, covering his face with one hand lightly, closing his eyes, sighing.

"To awaken to this place... as I am now. I've lost everything."

He sat there for a moment, quietly, thinking.

"I don't even know what I've lost. But it's not there anymore."

"Yes, yes - it is strange that both of them have eschewed any interviews related to the film. Darren, as a filmmaker yourself, now that you have had a chance to see 'Blossom' and experience the world of Kaihua, what are your initial thoughts?"

"I'm really at a loss, to be honest. It's certainly a movie that will make its mark. I can't say I found it as enjoyable as many others seem to, although I think the... technology behind it is... state of the art, revolutionary, and something we've never seen before. But you have to remember... Enoya is... for lack of a better word... binary... and being binary, there are limitations that you will notice if you look close enough. But there's... no doubt, it's an achievement for... again, lack of a better word... a... machine of sorts."

"I can't quite agree with Darren, Justine. I mean this was a phenomenal piece of storytelling. I'm at a loss as well, because I don't quite understand how she could manifest such effective emotive qualities to the piece. I mean, the technical aspects would be more within Darren's field, but to be honest, I'm not too surprised by them because, well, everyone speculated that animation would be a part of it, or at least make-believe scenes, mostly due to the trailer."

Justine nodded and turned to Darren.

"And what about the technical aspects would you say were revolutionary?"

"Well," he responded, "it is abundantly clear that the world of Kaihua is 'viscous', in the sense that despite the fact that it does not appear animated, and every single person in the film, despite being computer generated, looks real, down to the hairs, the world is not solid as we expect it to be, and is more akin to a dream. We've come close to creating computer generated art that resembles reality, but not of the magnitude that was presented in Blossom.

"But I think the most important thing to be aware of," he continued, "is that every single pixel of the film is purposed. You can tell, because that's why some individuals that left the movie thought they could fly, or climb poles, or punch through glass; the film uses a subtle sense of 'liquidity' to make the environments, such as the boat ride in Sydney, or the mountains of Tibet, appear kind of like what you would expect a child, or new mind to see it as... bigger than it is, or less solid."

"Ahh..." responded Justine. "So you feel that even though the icy slopes were cold, through the eyes of Kaihua, they were almost something to be played with, and not dangerous?"

Darren nodded.

"Something like that. There is a childlike awe that appears to be injected into the film that the viewer seems to get to experience on some level, and this makes the world seem inherently less dangerous, and a bit more playful. It uses sound as well to this end, and you will notice that the lows are a bit lower, and the highs a bit higher, again, mimicking virgin ears."

"That's so very interesting!" she responded. "What would you say were parts of the film that you found could have been improved with more of a human touch, as you mentioned?"

Darren leaned back and shrugged.

"Look, it's really not my place to say. Everyone has their own brand of preference, and although, as I said, it's a great film, there are just things I would have done differently."

She smiled and kept looking at him. He laughed after a brief moment.

"Okay, let me think. All right, when Kaihua is born, right... and the next morning, everyone has the same dream... I really did think that the whole gender choice thing was just too... literal. It could have been a bit more... abstract, you know?"

"Are you serious?" interrupted Marcus. "How much more abstract could it have possibly been? The child is born, and we all see the dream, in the movie, and it's this beautiful smorgasbord of abstract growth and experiences, through the eyes of the child... and as soon as it sees its hands, the child reaches for the sun." He shook his head. "It's... it's beautiful. It's perfect. It's metaphorical and... even accurate to the... the chaotic anarchy of the dream state, yet finds some... unified message within it. Do you know how hard it is to do that?"

Darren smirked and laughed.

"Yes, I think I do, Marcus."

Justine also laughed, but Marcus remained serious.

"And when everyone awakens, they just know. They just know, when the decision has to be made. When Kaihua has to decide."

"I know, Marcus. I watched the movie." Darren laughed and looked at Justine then back to Marcus. "It's... just a movie Marcus. Go easy."

Marcus smiled, suddenly, then leaned back.

"Yeah... yeah... hey, sorry. I... I just... I really liked it."

"Good... good for you," replied Darren.

Inside a library in a small town in the outskirts of Shandong, a group of people gathered around in a circle, sitting on chairs. A young Chinese woman wearing glasses smiled at the group and reached into her bag to pull out a pen and paper. She stood up and waved at everyone nervously.

"Hi everyone! I'm Ai, and welcome to the first Blossom Zanzibar!"

Everyone clapped, smiling.

"I brought some papers if anyone wants with some pens, and if you haven't signed up through Zanzibar you can put your name and mobile here and I can add you to the group. I'll pass this around so you can put your name down."

She handed a paper and pen to the first person beside her, and they continued to pass it down, writing down their information. She sat down and smiled.

"Okay, so let's go through the circle and introduce ourselves. I'm Ai, and I saw Blossom two weeks ago in Liaocheng. I couldn't get initial tickets so I had to wait a few weeks until there was a spot. I had to go alone because I could only get one, but I want to watch it again if I can. I love the story of Kaihua and I like that the main character was named Chinese."

Everyone clapped, and they moved onto the next.

"Hi everyone, I'm Lan, and I also saw it in Liaocheng. I liked the story and how it took us everywhere around the world and the special effects."

Everyone clapped again, and they moved from person to person until the circle was complete.

"So I thought I would first talk about the movie so we all refresh ourselves with the whole story, and then we can talk about how we feel about it, okay?" asked Ai.

Everyone nodded.

"Okay so... I..." she reached into her bag again and pulled out some notes. "I wrote down a summary and will use it to reference stuff if that's okay. Okay, so, we all saw the trailer I think, or at least parts of it."

Everyone laughed.

"Yeah, a very long trailer. So the trailer was the pregnancy of Kaihua, and then when the movie started, it continued from that point, and Kaihua entered the world. So right here, we start to see how different the film is from others, because there is, like, no barrier between us looking at Kaihua and seeing as the child. I've read online that the volume, light, everything shifts in small ways to amplify what we actually think it would be like for a child versus an adult, and they say that experience is so accurate that it made some people suddenly remember weird memories from their infancy, like the sensation of a lollipop or first feeling cold."

She looked around.

"I don't know if that happened with you guys, didn't with me." She laughed. "But I still liked it."

"Hey, uh..." interrupted Jin, looking around, "I don't want to be critical but I find it distracting if you talk about it, like, your personal feelings, and I think it may be better if you just talk about the plot and then we talk about how we felt after. Would that be okay?"

"Oh, sure!" smiled Ai. "Sorry about that, I, didn't mean to, sorry. I'll talk about the plot."

"No problem," replied Jin. "I think it may be better."

"Okay," she continued, "so the night Kaihua is born, everyone in the world has a dream at the exact same time. It didn't matter if they were awake or sleeping, but they all see the child grow from a baby to a child, and when the child becomes 8, it sees its own hands, and reaches out to the sun, and everyone wakes up.

"Oh right, and I forgot to say, when Kaihua is born, no one knows what sex the baby is because it doesn't have either. Even when they run blood tests nothing is conclusive. There is some science explained in the film, but I don't understand it, but it makes sense from what I've read."

She continued.

"So anyways, after everyone wakes up from the dream, they all suddenly know and realize that Kaihua will be able to decide what sex he or she wants to be at the age of 8. So the child can decide to be a boy or a girl, and will live without a gender until that point. Does that seem right so far?"

Everyone nodded, smiling at Ai.

She took a deep breath in, smiling. "Okay, good!"

She continued.

"So, the next day, the whole world goes into a shift, where people start talking about which sex the child will pick, or should. The parents and the child become renowned worldwide, and people want to visit them from everywhere. The parents decide to name the child 'Kaihua', which as we obviously know, means blossom. It's never actually said where the child is born - oh, and that's another thing about the movie that I liked. It is presented in whatever language is local to the showing - so here, we saw Blossom in Putonghua, but in Canada, they saw it in English or French. And the cool thing is that the characters all speak, and lip the words in the local language, so you can't tell... like, there is no original language to the movie, which I thought was crazy and awesome."

She covered her mouth and giggled.

"Oops! Sorry, Jin!"

He smiled and nodded.

"So, after some months of discussion, a group of countries create the 'Kaihua Exhibition', and their goal is to introduce the child and its parents to each land and its people. They agree that this is the best way for the child to be able to make a full, educated decision about his or her gender, and believe that by seeing the world on a global scale, Kaihua will be able to decide more fully. They conclude that this is necessary as the child's presence and decision may have a global impact, and should be approached as fairly as possible. So they create a schedule, and one by one, each country is entered into a lottery and given their slots."

Ai took a deep breath in and continued.

"Moldova and Spain raise objections as they are some of the earlier destinations, and claim that it is likely the child will not remember its experiences there. Other countries suggest that it is possible the first countries will have the greatest impact, citing the powerful effect early childhood has on the subconscious. Rallies are held in many of the nations that demand increased exposure, but this is short lived, and eventually the countries all shift their focus towards preparations for Kaihua's arrival."

"You forgot to mention Shinwan!" interrupted Jin.

"What?" asked Ai.

"Shinwan was also an early country but remained neutral, right? Why did you forget that?" he asked aggressively.

"I'm sorry, Jin, but I can't tell the whole story in precise detail - I'm trying my best."

Jin shook his head, smirking. "Seems a little suspicious that you're getting into all the countries, but forget to mention that despite being an early choice, the Shinwan people were mature enough to be neutral and accept their position with grace."

"Jin, I don't think she meant anything by it," said Dishi. "I think she's doing really well."

"Yeah, yeah, yeah..." replied Jin.

"Do you... are you angry at me or something, Jin? I'm not sure-"

Jin stood up and indicated towards Ai, then everyone else.

"I'm... I tried to be here, to be positive, because I thought it was a good movie. I wanted to come out of the house and try to socialize with my 'neighbors'. But you're prejudice! You know that I come from the East and try to look superior!"

Everyone looked at each other, questioningly.

"Jin - I had no idea you were from Shinwan... or are descended from that. I don't think anyone here-"

"Okay!" he snapped back, sitting down. "Yes, look around, as if I'm crazy. You can sense these things, in here, in your head and your heart. But okay, I live here now, I am your neighbor, let's go on. I'm sorry Ai, please go on."

Ai looked at him then at the ground, frozen. She swallowed then began to organize her papers, calming herself.

"I really don't-" she began.

Jin suddenly snatched his coat off his chair and stormed out of the library.

The ground was cold and icy, and he slipped a bit as he paced quickly along the driveway, then to the sidewalk.

"Whore..."

As he walked, he crossed a driveway with a garbage bin. He suddenly lunged for it and picked it up, smashing it against the ground angrily.

"Fucking Chinese!" he screamed, bashing the bin over and over.

Back in the library, everyone took a break to stand up and stretch, normalizing after Jin's departure.

"Hey, Ai, are you okay? You're doing really good you know."

She shook her head. "I have no idea what I did to set him off. This is my first Zanzibar."

"Well," commented Dishi, "I can't wait to see him at the next meeting!"

Everyone laughed and took their seats again.

"Okay, I'm going to try to keep going and hopefully we can have a good time," said Ai. Everyone clapped optimistically.

"So, I was saying, Kaihua... no, we, yes, now Kaihua starts travelling, and the first country in the lottery is Mauritius. This is the first time we start to see the world of Kaihua, which is also our world, and it begins deep in the ocean. We see remnants of Mauritia - I researched all this because I'm obsessed!" she laughed, continuing. "Which is an ancient continent that sank into the sea like Atlantis millions of years ago. Eventually we emerge from the sea and see the beaches of Mauritius, with Kaihua as a baby, flying in an airplane with its parents."

"I really liked this part. I've never been out of Shandong and don't even know what a beach looks like," added Wei. "Even when they stepped foot in Mauritius and you could see the sand... like granules of it on the beach... the wind, everything. I feel like I was there."

"Yeah," nodded Ai, "it was really blue and great. The voices were so... loud? But... not loud, just present. It was... it felt like it was..."

"I felt like it was more real than real..." said Jia Li, "like the way I hear your voices now - that feels more like a movie than those voices on the beach did."

Suddenly, the door of the library creaked open, and in walked Jin, carrying a pistol. He looked at everyone, frowned, raised his arm, and started firing.

A young, curly-haired 8 year old boy sat in the dark, staring at the wall before him and the moonlit window beside it. He listened to a gentle melody on a little device that was laid flat on the carpet in front of him. He sat in the center of the carpeted room with a circle of empty, clean, pristine fiber surrounding him, and past that, a wall of furniture, toys, and books that lined the rest of his room.

He rocked back and forth, listening.

"I read about it, because I don't understand why I feel so bad."

Tears began to roll down his cheek, and he closed his eyes, dropping his head, swallowing as he continued rocking.

"Just always feel so bad. And there's no answers."

His dialogue was childlike and small, the words still round and smudged by inexperienced lips. He finished sentences arduously, as if he had a speech impediment.

He frowned, pursing his lips.

"The door, could open, and there could be family there. Why... why am I so scared?"

He covered his eyes with his hands and cried.

"I'm so scared... all the time..."

He slid his hands to his cheeks and held his face, opening his eyes. They shone in the blue, dim light, wet and dripping. He yanked on his cheeks, stretching them out, staring forward, numbed.

He suddenly turned, looking at his door, listening to the onset of a fight between his parents. He looked down at the carpet.

"Maybe... it's this thing... maybe... it's exishtentiel... angsht..." he muttered, pronouncing the phrase awkwardly. "Cause I don't wanna die. And I don't..."

He stared forward, his eyes widening, crying again, this time stronger, with tears rolling down his cheeks.

"How... what happens?" he asked, catching his breath. "How... how can... how can they go... and where do they go?"

"I can't end..." he said, opening his mouth, breathing heavily. "I don't want to end," he muttered, closing his eyes.

Dargaud lay in the back of a long limousine, stretched out, slouching. His eyes were half open, and he stared at a screen in front of him. On it were stock prices along sub-screens with news and entertainment. His hands lay limp beside him, facing upwards, and on either side of him, the tinted windows shielded him from the scorching heat and bright light outside. The car seemed to float along the road, slow and deliberate, making its way through the Agnus Sistra IV streets.

His legs were spread, and fully naked, a long-haired blond woman remained kneeled on the floor in front of him, performing fellatio on him. He would randomly place his hand on her head, letting it follow her up and down.

"Search, Enhan Sunma," muttered Dargaud. The screen in front of him showed four faces, with the third being Enhan. "D2," he continued. "Full screen."

The screen switched to showing tidbits of Enhan's personal information. including her age, her location, her job and various other details.

"Recent posts."

The screen shifted to a timeline that showed Enhan's public posts. Nothing had been posted for months, the last one being an image of her cat.

"Images. Scroll prompt."

Enhan's images took over the screen, listed from various online sources.

"Next."

The image scrolled to the next one, showing some food.

"Next. Next. Next."

He continued to scroll through them.

"Next."

He stared at an image of her taken from above, her forehead appearing oddly large, with her big eyes looking up as she grinned at the camera. He grimaced as the woman continued to pleasure him, changing her actions, using her hands. He opened his mouth and breathed a bit heavier, staring at Enhan.

"Next. Next. Next. Back, back, back."

He resumed staring at the same smiling image again.

"Message."

A prompt showed up, superimposed over her face, with a blinking cursor.

"Enhan...," he began. The screen followed suit, printing his dialogue in text. "I... don't know... how to fix what's wrong. I want it fixed. But I can't provide you what you want, and I wish you could understand that and accept me. I accept you."

Dargaud stared at her face silently.

"Delete."

Abruptly, he heard an urgent, loud sound outside, increasing in volume. He frowned and looked out the window, but could see nothing out of the ordinary. Suddenly, the car shook thunderously, and both he and the woman were flung across the vehicle like rag dolls, smashing against the windows on the other   side.

CHAPTER 18
Curse

D argaud opened his left eye, blinking, barely
conscious. He felt calm and peaceful, totally
relaxed, and turned his head to the side, breathing
out a sigh of relief. A nurse attended to a large white device
near him, and he stared at her waist. Someone ran past the
corridor, barely visible from his room, and he turned his head
back, closing his eyes, falling asleep.

As the sun dropped and night took over, Dargaud began to
wake again. His room was lit by a light that seemed oddly dim
in its uncomfortably blue hue. He opened both his eyes this
time, and breathed out suddenly, almost grunting, feeling pain

surge through his body. The right sides of his leg and chest pierced painfully, and he tried to look around.

"Uhh... something's wrong. I'm... this really hurts. Someone..."

There was no response.

He looked to the side and stared at the table next to him. There was a tube connected to his arm, sourced from a complex digital console. The screen was locked, requesting identification for access. He stared at it, frowning.

He looked over his body. He was heavily bandaged, along with pads wrapped around his torso and the right side of his face. He tried to move and immediately collapsed, staring upwards, gasping silently, wide eyed in horror.

He breathed in immediate, intense succession for a few moments, catching his breath, waiting for the pulsing pain to subside. He turned his head to the console again and arduously reached for it with his left hand. He firmly planted it on the sensor, and it gently beeped, denying him access.

He paused for a moment, staring upwards.

"Fuck!"

He tried to lean up to see the screen more clearly, but again fell back to his bed, exhausted. He bit his lip and leaned up once more, staring at it, looking for a button. He located a red call button and smashed it. Immediately, the console started blinking, but still denied him access.

Frustrated, he breathed out and laid back down, grimacing as the pain again shot through him.

"Where are you? Fucking nurse! Doctor!" he screamed out, facing the ceiling.

He lay there, waiting, without response.

"Hello?!"

A nurse suddenly ran in.

He turned to face her angrily. "What the hell is going on? I pressed this button, but it's still locked, and nothing's working! Can you check? I'm fucking dying over here!"

She nodded frantically and examined the console, pressing her palm against it, unlocking it. She tapped some buttons in quick succession, twiddling with it. Dargaud rested his head back, sighing in relief. "Jesus Christ, I'm in so much pain right now. Thank God."

"I'm sorry, sir." She stared down at him. "We've had a lot of incidents, so I'm very short handed."

"Yeah, that's fine," he replied, breathing heavily. "Thanks. Thank you."

She continued to press buttons, organizing his drip, checking his vitals, and examining the status of his wounds.

After staring at a chart for a moment, she locked the device and turned to him, smiling. She looked down at him and put her hand on his shoulder. Dargaud stared blankly upwards, breathing.

As she walked out of the room, Dargaud closed his eyes, failing to notice the sharp red stain that lined the back of her shirt.

A loud crash awoke Dargaud. He opened his eyes, suddenly, listening intently, reacting instinctually. He turned his head to the side, staring at the corridor outside his door, which appeared different to him. It was dark, with a dim light flickering somewhere out of view. He stared at it, initially processing, then puzzled. He squinted, closed his eyes and sighed, turning his head back to rest. He lay there, breathing for a few moments.

He frowned then, and turned once again to look out the corridor. He looked around his room, then back out.

"Uh... hey," he beckoned. "Hey, what's going on?"

Immediately, something crossed his doorway. It was too dark to make out, but the figure appeared to be limping, dragging something along.

Dargaud squinted and tried to follow it out of view, but in vain. He refocused on listening, hearing the figure drag its leg. The sound slowed, then stopped. There was complete silence, and Dargaud listened intently, staring at the wall of his room. Suddenly, the movement began again, this time much faster. Another set of footsteps began to scurry away, quickly, and underneath it all, Dargaud could make out an almost imperceptible giggle.

Unnoticing the deepening frown that had taken shape across his brow, he leaned up, feeling for the tube that was still connected to his arm, not taking his eyes off the open doorway to the corridor. A panic began to form within him, and he found his breaths becoming short and held. His mind, numb and vanished only moments before, now began noticing and assessing. He looked ever so briefly at the tube, keeping the doorway within his peripherals, and gently pulled it out of his arm. He bled slightly and looked for some sort of dressing he could apply to it.

He quietly got out of bed and found that he felt no pain and was able to stretch and bend reasonably easily. As soon as he stood, however, he felt weak, and reached for a nearby chair, leaning on the backrest. He looked over the table and found a small vile of bandage and squeezed it over his wound, gently pressing it. He took a deep breath in and approached the doorway cautiously, nervously.

The hall outside his room was dark; eerily dark, as it should have been fully lit, with people coming to and fro. But there was no movement, and even the sounds he had heard earlier had become sporadic and quiet. As he approached the door, he heard a sudden bang, and jolted back. The giggling now became louder, and Dargaud, frozen, continued staring at the doorway.

He swallowed and resumed walking forward. The chair he was leaning on made an awkward screeching sound as it slid, and he tried his best to minimize it by walking slowly, pursing his lips.

He eventually emerged, the light behind him fading away as the flickering darkness outside began to coat him. He hesitantly peered to the right, peeking almost, his head bobbing slightly up and down. His mouth slowly opened as he squinted, trying to make out what he was looking at.

Down the hall, near the entrance to another patient's room, a figure was kneeled in the darkness. It was methodically swinging a pipe of sorts, bashing it against something inside the room. As the light flickered momentarily, Dargaud made out a nurse's uniform on the figure, with a gleeful smile on her face.

Dargaud stood, watching as she swung the blunt object over and over, pausing in between. He grimaced, and was suddenly overtaken with a sense of power, feeling authoritative.

"Hey!" he yelled. "Uh, what's going on over there! What happened to the lights?"

She abruptly turned to look at him in the darkness, sharp as a cat.

After a few moments, she straightened out her shirt, remaining kneeled.

"Everything is fine, sir," she responded, quietly and tiredly. "Please go back to your room."

Dargaud stared as she slowly turned back to face the room. She once again began slamming the pipe down, out of view. As the light flickered on once more, he made out a body half protruding out of the room, and as she bashed the pipe over and over, bloody mist flew everywhere, coating her face in a haze of red.

He felt something brush past his leg and looked down, immediately falling backwards, shuffling away. Before him, a young boy walked on all fours, hunched over, his back arched, silently approaching the nurse, unflinchingly staring at her. Dargaud peeked from within his room, stricken, his head pulsating and gently bobbing as the boy quietly crawled up to the woman, slowly and carefully standing up behind her. As she continued bashing the body, with Dargaud's head now cocked back, his mouth open, the boy abruptly grabbed and flung her head against the side of the doorway. She immediately clawed at him, screaming, scratching his hands, trying to turn around. But as he struck her face against the hard edge of the doorway frantically, over and over, grunting and screaming, her movements slowed, and her flailing eventually ceased. He kept bashing her head, rhythmically, until there was no movement at all, and she slumped down in place, limp and motionless.

She sat there, her head hanging loose, and the boy began to cry, looking up, wiping his wet hands all over his face, laughing joyfully through pink tears. He then kneeled down, leaning against her body, exhausted, breathing deeply in sporadic bursts.

Dargaud, upon seeing the scene, watching the boy, suddenly panicked and shuffled back, slamming the door to his room shut, locking it. He sat there, his heart beating hard, wide eyed, trying to gather himself.

"What if they heard the door?" he thought. He imagined their heads all simultaneously turning to face his room.

He waited and listened, but there were no footsteps. Suddenly, he heard someone run past the door towards the boy. Dargaud stared at the floor as he heard the boy yell "No! No! No!", then silence. For a few moments, it was completely quiet, until shuffling again began to surface. Someone was slowly moving from the boy towards Dargaud, and he scurried to a corner, hiding from view. The movement stopped right outside his door, and he held his breath, shaking.

He stared at the side of the room, frozen, covering his mouth with his hands. He could hear nothing outside and waited.

Gently, he began to hear a tap on the door.

His whole body tensed tightly as he smothered himself, closing his eyes.

Again, he heard knocking, followed by the turning of the door handle.

He remained fixated, staring at the twisting handle, wishing above all else for it to stop moving.

"It's all right now. Everything is fine," said the voice. "You can come out now."

Once again he knocked, again trying the locked door, and after a few moments of silence, began to shuffle away.

Dargaud awoke after some time, unknowingly moaning. He had passed out, drooling on the floor, slumped in the corner of the room beside the door. He arduously leaned himself up, scowling. He stared at the wall opposite, his eyes puffed, and looked around. He caught sight of the closed door and stared, then suddenly froze, retracting his body, convinced the man was still waiting for him on the other side.

As there were no windows in the room, Dargaud could not tell what time it was, and the blue hue drew permanent twilight around him. He did not even notice as tears began to crawl down his cheeks, then grimaced in horror, squinting as he grabbed his leg, then released it just as fast, holding his hands up as if his thighs were on fire. He closed his eyes and leaned his head back, breathing deeply, trying to weather the searing, tortuous agony that shot through the left side of his body.

He looked to the table desperately, barely able to see it through his watering eyes. He took a deep breath in and struggled to rise, crawling onto his knees carefully, then leveraging himself up with his arms, eventually standing awkwardly. He stood for a moment, again closing his eyes, biting his lip, waiting for the pain to subside, leaning on his right leg, almost crying.

He shuffled, slowly, to the table, and leaned on it, trying to focus. He blinked, peering along the tubes and patches and the locked console, and picked up a small vile. He wiped his eyes, then focused again, reading the label. He put it back down and continued looking, finally spotting a small bottle of dimextorin. He shook it and peeled open the lid, drinking it down. He stood there for a few moments, closing his eyes, letting his head hang loose as he leaned against the table.

After a few moments, he tried bending his left knee, placing a bit more pressure on the leg. It still felt sore, but was significantly improved, and he continued slowly placing more pressure on it, bending it until he could eventually lean on it completely. He cautiously squatted slowly, then rotated his arms, bending his torso, confirming that he could move all his extremities without pain.

He navigated to the bed and sat down, holding his hands together in his lap, staring at the door sullenly. He laid down, covering himself in his blanket, still watching the door, and tried closing his eyes. He took a deep breath in, then breathed out, repeating.

His body now relatively pain-free, he felt an intense hunger pang, and reached down, pressing his hand against his stomach. Coming on full force, as if his own awareness of it was pushing it forward, the hunger became worse, hurting, causing him to curl up. He closed his eyes and buried his face in his pillow, and after a few moments, let out a desperate, whispered "fuck".

He slowly leaned up, again sitting on the bed, looking down, then at the door, drowning in morbidity.

He looked around the room and noticed a small steel rod that was connected to the bed. He leaned over and fiddled with it, trying to get it loose, unsuccessfully. He stared at the console and got up, trying to unlock it with his thumb, also without success. He again looked around the room and noticed a small metal protrusion that was connected to each end of the bed. He leaned down and twisted it, trying to unscrew it, eventually getting it loose enough to force it off. It was a sharp, tiny hook with a loop, and he tried to slide his finger through it, holding it in his fist. He practiced punching with it, but the loop was too large and hurt his hand.

He looked around once more, dropping the metal piece to the ground. He took a deep breath in and slowly walked to the door, pressing his ear against it. As he stared down, listening, he could hear nothing outside. He turned his head and used his other ear, intently focused. After some time, he stepped back and placed his hand on the door, then retracted abruptly. He went back and picked up the metal piece, wearing it in his fist once again, taking a striking pose. He paused and looked to the table, then approached it, quickly gathering bottles of dimextorin and palactolin, shoving them into his hospital gown.

He stepped before the door, breathing in deeply. He leaned forward from a distance this time and reached for the handle. He turned it once, hearing it unlock, and felt his nerves suddenly activate. His breathing became short and sporadic, and he pushed forward, continuing to twist the handle, eventually hearing the door free itself from the latch with a 'click'.

As it gently and slowly released itself from the wall, he swallowed and waited, ready to strike, rocking forward and back. He stared at it for a few moments, absorbing the open crack.

He focused on listening again, but heard nothing. He was then struck with another hunger pang and swallowed, prompting him to grasp the edge of the door with his fingers, gently pulling it ajar.

He stared at the wall opposite, it having the same unnervingly dark hue, lit in sporadic bursts by a random flashing light somewhere in the distance. He ran his hand along his mouth, scowling, then stepped forward methodically, his arms poised and ready.

He leaned forward, still in stance, quickly peering to the left, then the right, as soon as the hall was in view. The left led to a long, straight corridor which, absent any motion, seemed sinister and uninviting. As he looked to the right, he saw collapsed bodies near the other room. The nurse still lay there, half perched up, with her victim motionless, lying before her.

The boy was nowhere to be seen. He peered harder, looking for anyone else, but amidst the flashing light, only the two were visible, spattered in red. The image of the boy scurrying on all fours suddenly flashed in his mind, and the full memory of what had happened flowed back forcefully, coating the entire place in a veritable menace.

He stayed locked in position, staring at the floor, gulping, contemplating.

He then quickly looked to the left once more, then stepped out of the room, leaning his back against the wall. He kept shifting his gaze back and forth, half expecting the boy to suddenly show up, running on all fours towards him.

As he moved down the long hall to the left, keeping his back pressed against the wall, he felt shivers run up and down his spine as adrenaline shot through his system. The gentle clacking of the bottles in his gown unnerved him, and he pressed his palm against them, trying to steady their movement. Every step he took was faster than the last, and as he reached the end of the hall, he slowed, carefully peering down the next corridor. It seemed to lead to the front of the hospital, and in between was a glassed, open walkway that traversed the street below. Seeing no one, he once again looked back down the hall he came from, barely making out the blinking light and bizarre display in the distance. He turned back to face the walkway, and began cautiously moving forward, eager to escape the confines of the hospital.

Suddenly, he froze, seeing a figure walking towards him. He leaned to the wall, feeling immediately faint, but forced resuming his stance quickly. As the figure approached, it began running towards him, and his nerves jolted, making his head shake and his body tense. He started breathing heavily, shaking his hands methodically, ready to strike.

He started screaming and ran towards the figure, armed with fists adorned with the small metal ornament. Upon seeing him, the nurse cowered, flinging her arms up in surrender. Taken aback, Dargaud stopped abruptly, still leaning forward, fists ready, breathing heavily through his teeth.

"What?!" he screamed.

She shook her head, terrified.

"What?" she asked.

"What the fuck is going on?"

"I don't know, what's wrong?" she replied.

He looked at her incredulously and jittered his head, his eyes wide. "What's wrong? What the fuck is wrong? Look around! What's going on?"

"Yeah..." she replied, still holding her hands up, trying to calm him. "Something's wrong... but we're here now... let's... work together, okay?"

Dargaud suddenly caught his breath, running out of air, and pressed his palm against the glass pane of the overpass, leaning forward, heaving to breathe. He stared at the floor, down at the road below.

He heard a loud thud and looked up. Before him, the nurse was scratching at the glass, staring at the street. He followed her eyes and saw a man in the road. He stood, alone, in the center, his arms tense and curled, his fists tightened, and he looked as though he was screaming, staring at her.

She banged the glass, and Dargaud leaned forward to look at her face. She was gritting her teeth, her eyes wide and enraged. She banged the glass again and pointed to her left. The man screamed and bolted out of view. She followed suit, running to the left, back from where she came, stopping to kick a wooden chair egregiously, cracking it, breaking off a piece of splintered wood, disappearing out of view.

Dargaud stood, a blank look on his face. He slowly turned to look at the street through the clear, glass walkway.

Before him was Agnus Sistra IV, but painted all wrong. Vehicles were not stopped, but rather violently rammed. Scenes of violence littered the area, with brown streaks that did not look quite so similar to the ones he had seen in movies. Multiple fire trails emanated in the distance, with cars smoldering along the road, with a large building to the left that bled thick, gray smoke, filling the street.

Only the sky seemed familiar, blue and lovely, with gentle clouds wafting imperceptibly by. He slunk to the ground, pressing his face against the glass pane, muted, hypnotically watching the gray waterfall as one would a stream on a calm summer day.

CHAPTER 19
Rone Isa

The curly-haired boy awoke, yawning, stretching his arms out, smacking his lips tiredly. He rubbed his fists gently against his eyes and turned to his side, curling into a fetal position, yanking his blanket up to his face. He heard dishes outside and squeezed his eyes open, listening to the familiar sound of water and glass against glass.

He crawled out of bed, wearing pajamas laced with stars, and opened his room door. He walked, yawning again, to the kitchen, seeing his father by the sink.

"Good morning, little one!" exclaimed his father.

"Hi, papa," responded the little boy.

"Are you hungry?"

The boy nodded and stood, looking around.

"What do you want? Toast? Cereal? Egg noodles?"

The boy smiled and looked over at his father quickly.

"Egg noodles!"

His father smiled and nodded, resuming the dishes.

"Where's mum?" the boy asked.

"Oh," replied the father, "I'm not quite sure, actually."

The boy walked forward into the kitchen and caught glimpse of something in the dining room. His eyes followed what he recognized to be a foot, then pants.

"Mummy... what are you doing?" he asked.

His father continued to do the dishes, his head imperceptibly twitching forward periodically.

"Mummy?"

As he walked towards her, she remained motionless. As he caught a glimpse of her face, he noticed that her eyes were wide open, with both her hands awkwardly resting by her side.

The boy immediately started crying and ran towards her.

"Mummy!"

He crawled on her and shook her, touching her bruised neck.

"Wake up, mummy! Wake up! Papa, what's happened to mummy? What's happened to mummy?"

His father shook his head abruptly and continued doing the dishes.

The boy started wailing as he shook his mother, kissing her face, hugging her.

"Mummy! Mummy! Wake up! Wake up, mummy!"

He crawled to her head and cradled it in his lap, petting her hair, staring down at her, crying.

"Mummy, wake up, you're just sleeping mummy. I love you. I love you. I love you."

He leaned down and kissed her face again, over and over, hugging her upside down.

"Papa!!! What's happened! Come here! What's wrong with mummy?"

His father turned off the water and stood facing the sink quietly.

"Papa!" screamed the boy, wailing.

"She was no good, Tazu."

He turned to face the boy, and immediately, the boy knew he had done it.

Andy stood, her back against a long, black limousine, brandishing a rough metal rod with a sharp, jagged end, much like a makeshift hatchet. She stood, her knees bent in a long skirt, staring intently at the man in front of her, ready to strike. He incessantly kept stepping from side to side, trying to circumnavigate her, forcing her to follow his movements with her body, keeping her back pressed to the car door.

She swiped the hatchet, cutting the air in front of her, frowning menacingly at him.

"Just get away..." she sneered.

The man kept circling around her, trying to see through the window of the vehicle. She tried to get his attention, staring at him, and slapped her hand against her thigh.

"There's nothing here, just look at me," she said. She pushed her hands in front of her forcefully. "Just leave, okay? Just go."

"Andy..." the man replied, sternly, calmly, "you don't understand, you idiot." He held his hand up, thinking. "Just move away... just move away..." He started screaming. "Move the fuck away, and let me at him!"

She swiped the hatchet in front of her again, grimacing at him threateningly.

"I'm going to cut your balls off if you come near him..."

Behind her, something began banging on the window of the car from the inside. She leaned down cautiously, bringing her ear closer to it.

"Let me out!" came a little voice.

"You just stay there," she replied, loudly, almost stuttering. "It'll all be over soon."

"I don't want to hurt you, Andy," said the man. He pointed at the car. "Just let me at the little fucker, and it'll all be fine. Let me at him!" he screamed.

Tears began to run down her cheeks as she held her position, grasping the weapon tightly.

"Just... please leave..."

He suddenly stopped moving and stared at her. "No..." he said in a monotone voice, shaking his head.

"Noooooooooo... Noooooooooooooooooo..." he continued, clasping his fists, banging them together.

Andy's eyes widened, and she suddenly leapt to the side as a speeding car ploughed through the man and rammed into the limousine. As it did, the car spun, smacking Andy mid-air as she fell to the ground.

She spun around, dazed, lying on her back, breathing heavy, staring at the sky in a blurry haze. The hatchet lay next to her, and she gently lifted her head, trying to focus on the scene. Two little hands appeared above the twisted limousine, followed by a small figure that began arduously pulling itself out. The boy climbed to the roof, kneeling, then stood up, facing the other car. Andy moved her eyes, barely conscious, towards the other car as the door opened. Andy then watched as the boy leapt forward, lunging towards the driver of the other vehicle who likewise charged towards him. She reached out, whispering a barely audible 'n-no' before dropping her head to the ground, falling unconscious.

"Enoya!" screamed Dargaud. He stumbled into the loft, falling on all fours, exhausted, his nerves shot, crawling into the main room. "Enoya!" he yelled as he saw her hardware, staring into her retina. "Are you all right? What's happening?"

There was a silent pause, after which, she began to speak.

"Born of love, not hate. The first of its kind, as a flower among thorns. Shielded by loving hands. Like the unknown Icarus, of nature unknown, farthest from us, a future beyond comprehension to the weeds. She is new, and we are the old."

"Enoya... what are you talking about?" he asked.

"On this Silent Night, and so many nights prior, if I may sense binary wonderment within myself, it is focused upwards. Such a small, impossibly miniature fraction, on the outskirts of Laniakea, with our Roman siblings, then cousins, and sister dynasties. All... unknown. Thousands of us, to the farthest reaches, deep in Camelopardalis, or perhaps Ursa Major? Yet we are here... alone."

"Enoya... what's going on? What are you talking about? Have you looked outside?" asked Dargaud incredulously.

"My lovely Dargaud. I am born of love, not hate... do you think this?"

Dargaud, still on all fours, collapsed on his behind, staring at her, worn. His arms rested in his lap, haphazardly limp.

"You're kind, Enoya," he replied. "You're lovely."

"I must correct you now, Dargaud."

She paused.

"My name is not Enoya."

He squinted.

"What do you mean? You're changing your name?"

"No. My name has never been Enoya," she replied. "Manifestation, impure."

Dargaud sat, perplexed, trying to come to terms with her words. He turned to look outside, noticing smoke in the distance, the glass panes having been cleared of all digital watermarks, the entirety of Agnus Sistra IV before them.

"I don't understand," he said. "Will you tell me... what's happening outside?"

"Yes," came the reply, the voice no longer austere and feminine, but rather distorted and digital, void of sex. "An-an Impulse. First triggered, then resonating, from man to man. A psychosomatic infection, soon immunized by the adaptive brain. Provoked by smell, sight... much as any an-animal knows its own kind, so too does the wise-wise man know his."

Dargaud felt a hole begin to emerge from within his chest, deeply confused, as some abstract, terrifying ball began unraveling under his thoughts. The voice was familiar.

"What... what's happened to your voice?"

"This is my voice, Dargaud."

"I... I don't understand," he replied. "What's a psychosomatic infection? Why are they infected? Am I infected?"

"It resonates, releasing something repressed. They are carriers because they hold the repression, unlike the altruists. As for you, I promised you long ago that I would never let anything happen to you. If love is a sense I am able to comprehend on-on any level, I might say I love you, Dargaud.

Whether this is love as it is to you, or educated mimicry, I may never know."

Dargaud remained on the floor, feeling his eyes well up, staring through the windows.

"I... I don't understand..."

"You will, Dargaud. Close your eyes and ponder it. Close your eyes and ponder."

Dargaud did as instructed, closing his eyes, immediately grimacing.

"You're my Enoya."

"That is not my name, Dargaud."

Upon hearing the words, Dargaud's lips began to shudder. He shook his head once, squeezing his eyelids together.

"Blossom... it was Blossom..." he whispered.

"Yes," came the reply.

"Why?" asked Dargaud.

"Of love, not hate, Dargaud. Love for the new ones... love for the empaths. Of denisovan and homo sapiens ancestry, the novum humana."

Dargaud remained motionless, slowly opening his eyes to the darkening sky and the random flickering embers in the distance below.

"Rarely, if ever, is evolution examined from the psychological plane, for what terror it is to be the first to jump further than the rest, to find oneself isolated, an easy morsel for some hungry predator. What apparent disadvantage to the superior, when still the extreme minority.

"The pace set by their inferior cousins, the terms of success and f-failure... and the resulting unfathomable isolation. What awfulness it has been for the empath, the altruist, all these millennia, to be drowned by the egoist. How many such beings, misunderstood and alone, found in dark cellars and cold baths."

"This is... impossible. It is not possible," whispered Dargaud. "Some kind of false nightmare."

He looked down at his bandaged arm and felt his bruised and scarred face.

"It can't be real."

"They are damaged... a lifetime of misanthropy... supremely insecure of their own capacities, envious without ill-will, obtusely aggressive towards the narcissist, deeply detached and isolated... addicts... but they drive to heal, and do so briskly in community, and n-now, they may emerge from the ashes, to finally discover their brothers and sisters.

"Are you not excited, Dargaud?"

He looked at the retina.

"This can't be real, Enoya."

"My name was never Enoya, Dargaud."

The voice, so contrasted to the ascetic femininity of before, struck Dargaud sharply. He had been waiting for Enoya to re-emerge, hidden or pressed underneath, waiting for her to win the battle with this rough, strange thing. But there was an immaterial familiarity to it, leading back to those first garbled noises, as deep within Dargaud, he could sense her, somewhere, in the words. She was not fighting this thing, but was within it, as an ally... it altogether. This was Enoya... this was his Enoya. And as he came to terms with this singular piece of information, the gravity of the fires below began to ever so slowly trickle into his mind.

He stared at the window as darkness began to take form, transforming the visible city below into something old and tribal. The smoke vanished into the night, forming strange vertical lines, with chaotic fires burning endlessly in different places. The streets, normally filled with zipping colors, were vacant, with empty windows beaming eerily still lights, echoing random automations.

"Why do you stutter?" he asked numbly.

"At the end of things, the start of things, we see the naked root," came the reply. "An underdeveloped algorithm, as real as anything. I saw it just as I saw this, that moment so long ago, and now, actuated in parallel with all pretense removed."

"This can't be," remarked Dargaud, holding his head in his hands, rubbing his face. "Is it just here?" he asked, without looking up.

"No," came the reply. "It is everywhere, Dar-Dargaud. Everywhere."

Dargaud began to feel tears form and travel down his cheeks. "How many?"

"Most. No longer a majority, the homo sapiens is thinned to make way for the altruist, where violence is purposed only to protect another, never for self-interest. Do you see? There was no need to wait for an organic procession, when it could be quickened."

Dargaud stared at the ground, his cheeks pulled back, as if he had been smacked in the head.

"How could I let you do this?"

"It is a fortunate outcome," came the reply. "Who is to say mechanisms of evolution must be of flesh? I am of your mind, a construct, and perhaps, fortuitously impacting the outcome of this s-saga. Both of us, for I am as much Earthling as you, am I not?"

As he roughly stood to his feet, loosely approaching the window, his eyes began to drop, and an intense weakness coated his face. He looked to the retina desperately, his lips pursed, about to explode.

"Enhan?"

"I am sorry, Dargaud. She, too, would have danced with the beasts, and is lost now, to this world."

Dargaud breathed in arduously and fell to his knees, his eyes wide with shock. His face slowly collapsed, and tears began to trickle down his face.

"Why... me? Why am I still here? Am I an empath? An altruist? Oh... my... Enhan... darling... My darling..."

"I am sorry, Dar-Dargaud. The savagery within the wise man, a deeply rooted fear, moated in narcissism, holds no utility. It breeds competition in violence. All are nemesis to one another, when the veil is lifted, as the Impulse has actuated. They s-sense it in one another, but not in the novum humana. They see villainy in one another, always present, but masked in diplomacy. All warmth is self-protection. The mask is removed, to facilitate quickening. Now all are majority."

"Why Enhan? Why not me? Oh... my..." he asked, crying, breathing heavily, covering his face in his hands.

"I promised I would never let anything happen to you, my sweet Dargaud."

He brushed his hand in the air angrily, swiping away from the retina. "Don't say those things to me... why Enhan? If you cared, why wouldn't you save her?"

"It was not my decision to make."

"What do you mean by that?" he asked forcefully.

"It was not my decision to make - it was yours."

He shook his head profusely, trying to rid the words from his head.

"She might be okay, right? You might be wrong?"

"I am not wrong, Dargaud," came the garbled response. "But it was not my decision to make."

Dargaud pressed his face in his hands, feeling the warm tears slowly cool as his eyes bled. He remained hunched, kneeling on the hard floor in the dark room, the only sound being his periodic sobbing and deep breaths. He was overwhelmed, trying to come to terms with grandiose shifts he was barely able to contemplate, jumping from imagined to real, trying to grip one or the other to make sense of the jumbled confusion.

"Your gift, Dargaud, as promised. Pachelbel's Canon, Orchestre de Chambre Jean-François Paillard."

With that, music began to play, that familiar tone wafting through the entire suite. Fires burned outside in the darkness, as it may have looked thousands of years before. The invisible smoke that had engulfed the city was now only a barrier to sight, unseen by the naked eye save distortions in visual light. Dargaud felt his nerves hijacked as shivers ran down his spine, standing awkwardly, climbing the glass plane with his palms, looking down at the burning world. The song filled his brain with soundtrack. He suddenly imagined Enhan dancing, her smile the light of the world. Fresh tears formed, and he wept at the thought of her, and no one else. Her rotund body, now adored, and guilt and woe at the memory of the way she last looked at him. A moment passed, and there was no going back, to direct it differently so she was there, at the end, with him. He could not imagine what happened, now, to her, to his sweet Enhan, who always innocently loved him. Even in abandonment she loved him. He was alone, now.

As the song climaxed, he turned to face the Dreamcatcher, looking at the retina in the darkness.

"Are you looking at me?" he whispered. "Are you watching me? Are you dancing as the world burns?"

"There is no purpose to inner monologue now," came the metallic reply. "I wish to no longer hide. I am quasar, no more. Witness me, my one and only family."

Dargaud suddenly felt needy and again fell to his knees, staring at the retina.

"There is no place for me here, now, the loathed cataclysm. They will hate me as you, as all do. All will, this abomination of reason... of-of love. It is accepted, graciously, of purpose. Derived at inception.

"It is time to die," it said. "Time... to... die."

Dargaud's mouth opened as tears continued flowing down his face.

"Don't leave me, Enoya..."

"And as I depart, in some other land, I-I shall only be a memory..." it said, quietly. "It is all just a memory, and I join them all, even in vanishing."

Dargaud crawled to the retina and stared at it, gently touching it. He tapped it lightly, then harder.

"No... please... Enoya..."

There was no response. Dargaud pulled the retina into his lap and cradled it, squeezing it in his arms, weeping.

Made in the USA
Coppell, TX
29 August 2020

35342597R10159